"I'm

From what I've heard," Grace went on, "Cole was the workaholic, Dex, the playboy. Aren't you supposed to be the Hunter brother with a conscience?"

"I grew up," Wynn replied.

"Hardened up."

"And yet you're captivated by my charm."

Her lips twitched. "I wouldn't say that."

"So I dreamed that you came home with me three nights ago?"

"I was feeling self-indulgent. Guess we connected."

"In case you hadn't noticed, we still do."

"I can't regret the other night." She let out a breath. "But, I'm not interested in pursuing anything... rekindling any flames. It's not a good time."

Wynn felt his smile waver before firming back up. "I don't recall asking."

"So, that hand sliding toward my behind, pressing me against you...I kind of took that as a hint."

* * *

One Night, Second Chance
is part of The Hunter Pact series:
One powerful family, countless dark secrets

* * *

If you're on Twitter,
tell us what you think of Harlequin Desire!
#harlequindesire

Dear Reader,

Not only do I believe in love—true love—I believe in love at first sight. I'm not saying that the parties involved are necessarily aware at the time what is happening, but that forces greater than conscience and planning are at work, and working fast.

But when two people meet and connect in a way that changes them—encourages and buoys them like never before—perhaps the cosmos is trying to tell them something profound. Something "once in a lifetime."

When Grace Munroe meets Wynn Hunter, the tortured younger brother (and my favourite!) from this series, she is inexplicably drawn. They've met before, so long ago in their childhoods that neither recognizes the other. As adults, however, they will never forget their first remarkable night together, even when the very last thing either one needs or wants is to get involved.

Meanwhile, Wynn's oldest brother, Cole, is planning a wedding, the life of their media magnate father is still in danger and all kinds of betrayals are simmering beneath the surface of the families that comprise The Hunter Pact.

Hope you enjoy!

Best wishes,

Robyn Grady

ONE NIGHT, SECOND CHANCE

—

ROBYN GRADY

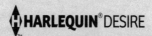

HARLEQUIN® DESIRE

Recycling programs
for this product may
not exist in your area.

ISBN-13: 978-0-373-73305-7

ONE NIGHT, SECOND CHANCE

Copyright © 2014 by Robyn Grady

All rights reserved. Except for use in any review, the reproduction or utilization of this work in whole or in part in any form by any electronic, mechanical or other means, now known or hereafter invented, including xerography, photocopying and recording, or in any information storage or retrieval system, is forbidden without the written permission of the publisher, Harlequin Enterprises Limited, 225 Duncan Mill Road, Don Mills, Ontario M3B 3K9, Canada.

This is a work of fiction. Names, characters, places and incidents are either the product of the author's imagination or are used fictitiously, and any resemblance to actual persons, living or dead, business establishments, events or locales is entirely coincidental.

This edition published by arrangement with Harlequin Books S.A.

For questions and comments about the quality of this book, please contact us at CustomerService@Harlequin.com.

® and TM are trademarks of Harlequin Enterprises Limited or its corporate affiliates. Trademarks indicated with ® are registered in the United States Patent and Trademark Office, the Canadian Trade Marks Office and in other countries.

Printed in U.S.A.

ROBYN GRADY

was first contracted by Harlequin in 2006. Her books feature regularly on bestsellers lists and at award ceremonies, including the National Readers' Choice Awards, the Booksellers' Best Awards, CataRomance Reviewers' Choice Awards and Australia's prestigious Romantic Book of the Year.

Robyn lives on Australia's gorgeous Sunshine Coast where she met and married her real-life hero. When she's not tapping out her next story, she enjoys the challenges of raising three very different daughters, going to the theater, reading on the beach and dreaming about bumping into Stephen King during a month-long Mediterranean cruise.

Robyn knows that writing romance is the best job on the planet and she loves to hear from her readers! You can keep up with news on her latest releases at www.robyngrady.com.

This book is dedicated to Holly Brooke.
I'm so very proud of you, baby. Aim for the stars!

Prologue

Turning her back on the wall-to-wall mirror, Grace Munroe unzipped and stepped out of her dress. She slipped off her heels—matching bra and briefs, too—before wrapping herself in a soft, scented towel. But when she reached the bathroom door, a chill rippled through her, pulling her up with a start.

She sucked down a breath—tried to get enough air.

I'm an adult. I want this.

So relax.

Let it go.

A moment later, she entered a room that was awash with the glow from a tall corner lamp. She crossed to the bed, drew back the covers and let the towel drop to her feet. She was slipping between the sheets when a silhouette filled the doorway and a different sensation took hold. She hadn't been in this kind of situation before—and never would be again. But right now, how she wanted this.

How she wanted *him*.

Moving forward, he shucked off his shirt, undid his belt. When he curled over her, the tip of his tongue rimmed one nipple and her senses flew into a spin.

His stubble grazed her as he murmured, "I'd like to know your name."

She didn't wince—only smiled.

"And I'd like us under this sheet."

This evening had begun with a walk to clear her thoughts; since returning to New York, she'd been plagued by memories and regrets.

Passing a piano bar, she was drawn by the strains of a baby grand and wandered in to take a seat. A man stopped beside her. Distinctly handsome, he filled out his tailored jacket in a way that turned women's heads. Still, Grace was ready to flick him off. She hadn't wanted company tonight.

To her surprise, he only shared an interesting detail about the tune being played before sipping his drink and moving on. But something curious about his smile left its mark on her. She felt a shift beneath her ribs—a pleasant tug—and her thinking did a one-eighty.

Calling him back, she asked if he'd like to join her. Ten minutes. She wasn't staying long. Slanting his head, he began to introduce himself, but quickly she held up a hand; if it was all the same to him, she'd rather not get into each other's stories. Each other's lives. She saw a faint line form between his brows before he agreed with a salute of his glass.

For twenty minutes or so, they each lost themselves in the piano man's music. At the end of the break, when she roused herself and bid him good-night, her stranger said he ought to leave, too. It seemed natural for them to walk together, discussing songs and sports, and then food and the theater. He was so easy to talk to and laugh with... There was almost something familiar about his smile, his voice. Then they were passing his building and, as if they'd known each other for years, he asked if she'd like to come up. Grace didn't feel obliged. Nor did she feel uncertain.

Now, in this bedroom with his mouth finding hers, she wasn't sorry, either. But this experience was so far from her norm. Was it progress or simply escape?

A year ago, she'd been in a relationship. Sam was a decorated firefighter who respected his parents—valued the community. Nothing was too much for his family or friends. He had loved her deeply and, one night, had proposed. Twelve months on, a big part of Grace still felt stuck in that time.

But not right now. Not one bit.

As her stranger's tongue pushed past her lips, the slow-working rhythm fed a hunger that stretched and yawned up inside of her. When he broke the kiss, rather than wane, the steady beating at her core only grew. She was attracted to this man in a way she couldn't explain—physically, intellectually...and on a different level, too. She would have liked to see him again. Unfortunately, that wasn't possible. This was all about impulse, sexual attraction—a fusion of combustible forces.

A one-night stand.

And that's how it needed to stay.

One

"Beautiful, isn't she?"

Wynn Hunter gave the older man standing beside him a wry grin. "Hate to tell you, but that bridesmaid's a little young for you."

"I would hope so." Brock Munroe's proud shoulders shucked back. "She's my daughter."

Wynn froze; his scalp tingled. Then he remembered to breathe. As his mind wheeled to fit all the pieces together, he swallowed and then pushed out the words. Brock had three daughters. Now it struck Wynn which one this was.

"That's *Grace*?"

"All grown up."

Brock didn't need to know just *how* grown up.

Had Wynn suspected the connection three nights ago, he would never have taken her back to his Upper East Side apartment—not so much out of respect for Brock, who was a friend of his father, Australian media mogul and head of Hunter Enterprises Guthrie Hunter, but because Wynn had despised Grace Munroe when they were kids. She'd made his blood boil. His teeth grind.

How could he have enjoyed the single best evening of sex in his life with that girl—er, woman?

"Grace gets her looks from her mother, like the other two," Brock went on as music and slow-spinning lights drifted around the Park Avenue ballroom, which was decked out for tonight's wedding reception. "Remember the vacation we all spent together? That Colorado Christmas sure was a special one."

Brock had met Guthrie as a Sydney University graduate vacationing at the newly opened Vail Resort. Over the years, they'd kept in touch. When the Munroes and Hunters had got together two decades later, Wynn had turned eight. Whenever he and his older brothers had built a snowman outside of the chalet the two families had shared, Grace and Wynn's younger sister Teagan had conspired to demolish it. Back then, Wynn's angel of a mother had still been alive. She'd explained that the six-year-olds had simply wanted to join in. Be included.

Now Wynn ran Hunter Publishing, the New York-based branch of Hunter Enterprises. Until recently, he had always prided himself on being an affable type. But that Christmas day, when Grace had tripped him up then doubled over with laughter as his forehead had smacked the snow—and the rock hidden underneath—he'd snapped. While she'd scurried inside, pigtails flying, Wynn's brother Cole had struggled to hold him back.

So many years had passed since then and yet, in all his life, Wynn doubted anyone had riled him more than that pug-nosed little brat.

But since then, her mousey pigtails had transformed into a shimmering wheat-gold fall. And her lolly-legs in kiddies' jeans had matured into smooth, endless limbs. He recalled that pest from long ago who had relentlessly poked and teased, and then remembered his mouth working over hers that amazing night they'd made love. When they'd struck up a conversation at that Upper East Side piano bar, Grace couldn't possibly have known who he was.

Could she?

"How's your father and that situation back in Australia?" Brock asked as Grace continued to dance with her partnered groomsman and other couples filled the floor. "We spoke a couple of months back. All that business about someone trying to kill him? Unbelievable." Brock crossed his tuxedo-clad arms and shook his head. "Are the authorities any closer to tracking down the lowlife responsible?"

With half an eye on Grace's hypnotic behind as she swayed around in that sexy red cocktail number, Wynn relayed some details.

"A couple of weeks after my father's vehicle was run off the road, someone tried to shoot him. Thankfully the gunman missed. When Dad's bodyguard chased him on foot, the guy ran out in front of a car. Didn't survive."

"But wasn't there another incident not long after that?"

"My father was assaulted again, yes." Remembering the phone call he'd received from a livid Cole, Wynn's chest tightened. "The police are on the case but my brother also hired a P.I. friend to help."

Brandon Powell and Cole went back to navy-cadet days. Now Brandon spent his time cruising around Sydney on a Harley and running his private-investigation and security agency. He was instinctive, thorough and, everyone agreed, the right man for the job.

As one song segued into another, the music tempo increased and the lights dimmed more. On the dance floor, Grace Munroe was limbering up. Her moves weren't provocative in the strictest sense of the word. Still, the way she arranged her arms and bumped those hips… Well, hell, she stood out. And Wynn saw that he wasn't alone in that impression; her first dance partner had been replaced by a guy who could barely keep his hands to himself.

Wynn downed the rest of his drink.

Wynn didn't think Grace had noticed him yet among the three hundred guests. Now that he was aware of their shared background, there was less than no reason to hang around until she did. It was way too uncomfortable.

Wynn gestured toward the exit and made his excuse to Brock "Better get going. Early meeting tomorrow."

The older man sucked his cheeks in. "On a Sunday? Then again, you must be run off your feet since Hunter Publishing acquired La Trobes two years ago. Huge distribution."

Brock was being kind. "We've also shut down four publications in as many years." As well as reducing leases on foreign and national bureaus.

"These are difficult times." Brock grunted. "Adapt or die. God knows, advertising's in the toilet, too."

Brock was the founding chairman of Munroe Select Advertising, a company with offices in Florida, California and New York. Whether members of the Munroe family helped run the firm, Wynn couldn't say. The night he and Grace had got together, they hadn't exchanged personal information…no phone numbers, employment details. Obviously no names. Now curiosity niggled and Wynn asked.

"Does Grace work for your company?"

"I'll let her tell you. She's on her way over."

Wynn's attention shot back to the floor. When Grace recognized him, her smile vanished. But she didn't turn tail and run. Instead, she carefully pressed back her bare shoulders and, tacking up a grin, continued over, weaving her way through the partying crowd.

A moment later, she placed a dainty hand on Brock's sleeve and craned to brush a kiss on his cheek. Then she turned her attention toward Wynn. With her head at an angle, her wheat-gold hair cascaded to one side. Wynn recalled the feel of that hair beneath his fingers. The firm slide of his skin over hers.

"I see you've found a friend," she said loud enough to be heard over the music.

Brock gave a cryptic smile. "You've met before."

Her focus on Wynn now, Grace's let's-keep-a-secret mask held up. "Really?"

"This is Wynn," her father said. "Guthrie Hunter's third boy."

Her entrancing eyes—a similar hue to her hair—blinked twice.

"Wynn?" she croaked. "Wynn *Hunter*?"

"We were reminiscing," Brock said, setting his empty champagne flute on a passing waiter's tray. "Remembering the time we all spent Christmas together in Colorado."

"That was a long time ago." Gathering herself, Grace pegged out one shapely leg and arched a teasing brow. "I don't suppose you build snowmen anymore?"

Wynn deadpanned. "Way too dangerous."

"Dangerous…" Her puzzled look cleared up after a moment. "Oh, I remember. You were out in the yard with your brothers that Christmas morning. You hit your head."

He rubbed the ridge near his temple. "Never did thank you for the scar."

"Why would you do that?"

Seriously?

"You tripped me."

"The way I recall it, you fell over your laces. You were always doing that."

When Wynn opened his mouth to disagree—six-year-old Grace had stuck out her boot, plain and simple—Brock stepped in.

"Grace has been friends with the bride since grade school," the older man offered.

"Jason and I were at university together in Sydney," Wynn replied, still wanting to set straight that other point.

"Linley and Jason have been a couple for three years," Grace said. "I've never heard either one mention you."

"We lost touch." Wynn added, "I didn't expect an invitation."

"Seems the world is full of surprises."

While Wynn held Grace's wry look, Brock picked up a less complicated thread.

"Wynn runs the print arm of Hunter Enterprises here in New York now." He asked Wynn, "Is Cole still in charge of your broadcasting wing in Australia?"

Wynn nodded. "Although he stepped back a bit. He's getting married."

"Cole was always so committed to the company. A workaholic, like his dad." Brock chuckled fondly. "Glad he's settling down. Just goes to show—there's someone for everyone."

It seemed that before he could catch himself, Brock slid a hesitant look his daughter's way. Grace's gaze immediately dropped. He made a point of evaluating the room before sending a friendly salute over to a circle of friends nearby.

"I see the Dilshans. Should go catch up." Brock kissed his daughter's cheek. "I'll leave you two to get reacquainted."

As Brock left, Wynn decided to let them both off the hook. As much as this meeting was awkward, their interactions three nights ago had felt remarkably right. Details of that time had also been private and, as far as he was concerned, would remain that way.

"Don't worry," he said, tipping a fraction closer. "I won't let on that you and I were already reintroduced."

She looked amused. "I didn't think you'd blurt out the fact that we picked each other up at a bar."

She really didn't pull any punches.

"Still don't want to get into each other's stories?" he asked.

"As it turns out, we already know each other, remember?"

"I didn't mean twenty years ago. I'm talking about now."

Her grin froze before she lifted her chin and replied. "Probably best that we don't."

He remembered her father's comment about there being a person for everyone and Grace's reaction. He recalled how she'd wanted to keep their conversation superficial that night. His bet? Grace Munroe had secrets.

None of his business. Hell, he had enough crap of his own going down in his life. Still, before they parted again, he was determined to clear something up.

"Tell me one thing," he said. "Did you have any idea who I was that night?"

She laughed. "There, see? You *do* have a sense of humor."

As she turned away, he reached and caught her wrist. An electric bolt shot up his arm as her hair flared out and her focus snapped back around. She almost looked frightened. Not his intention at all.

"Dance with me," he said.

Those honeyed eyes widened before she tilted her chin again. "I don't think so."

"You don't want the chance to trip me up again?"

She grinned. "Admit it. You were a clumsy kid."

"You were a brat."

"Be careful." She eyed the fingers circling her wrist. "You'll catch girl germs."

"I'm immune."

"Don't be so sure."

"Trust me. I'm sure."

He shepherded her toward the dance floor. A moment later, when he took her in his arms, Wynn had to admit that though he'd never liked little Gracie Munroe, he sure approved of the way this older version fit so well against him. Surrounded by other couples, he studied her exquisite but indolent face before pressing his palm firmly against the small of her back.

Dancing her around in a tight, intimate circle, he asked, "How you holding up?"

"Not nauseous…yet."

"No driving desire to curl your ankle around the back of mine and push?"

"I'll keep you informed."

He surrendered a grin. He just bet she would.

"Where's your mother tonight?"

Her cheeky smile faded. "Staying with my grandmother. She hasn't been well."

"Nothing serious, I hope."

"Pining. My grandfather passed away not long ago. He was Nan's rock." Her look softened more. "I remember my parents going to your mother's funeral a few years back."

His stomach gave a kick. Even now, memories of his father failing due to lack of sleep from his immeasurable loss left a lump in Wynn's throat the size of an egg. The word *saint* had been tailor-made for his mom. She would never be forgotten. Would always be missed.

But life had gone on.

"My father married again."

She nodded, and he remembered her parents had attended the wedding. "Is he happy?"

"I suppose."

A frown pinched her brow as she searched his eyes. "You're not convinced."

"My stepmother was one of my mother's best friend's daughters."

"Wow. Sounds complicated."

That was one way to put it.

Cole and Dex, Guthrie's second-oldest son, had labeled their father's second wife a gold digger, and worse. Wynn's motto had always been Right Is Right. But not everything about Eloise Hunter was black or white. Eloise was, after all, his youngest brother Tate's mom. With his father's stalker still on the loose, little Tate didn't need one ounce more trouble in his life, particularly not nasty gossip concerning one of his parents running around.

Out of all his siblings, Wynn loved Tate the best. There was a time when he'd imagined having a kid just like him one day.

Not anymore.

Wynn felt a tap on his shoulder. A shorter man stood waiting, straightening his bow tie, wearing a stupid grin.

"Mind if I cut in?" the man asked.

Wynn gave a curt smile. "Yeah, I do."

With pinpricks of light falling over the dance floor in slow motion, Grace tsked as he moved them along. "That wasn't polite."

Wynn only smiled.

"He's a friend," she explained.

What could he say? *Too bad.*

She looked at him more closely. "I'm confused. From what I've heard, Cole was the workaholic, Dex, the playboy. Aren't you supposed to be the Hunter brother with a conscience?"

"I grew up."

"Hardened up."

"And yet you're captivated by my charm."

Her lips twitched. "I wouldn't say that."

"So I dreamed that you came home with me three nights ago?"

She didn't blush. Not even close.

"I was feeling self-indulgent. Guess we connected."

"In case you hadn't noticed," his head angled closer, "we still do."

Her hand on his shoulder tightened even as she averted her gaze. "I've never been in that kind of situation before."

He admitted, "Neither have I."

"I can't regret the other night." She let out a breath. "But, I'm not interested in pursuing anything…rekindling any flames. It's not a good time."

He felt his smile waver before firming back up.

"I don't recall asking."

"So, that hand sliding toward my behind, pressing me in against the ridge in your pants… I kind of took that as a hint." Her smile was thin. "I'm not after a relationship, Wynn. Not right now. Not of any kind."

He'd asked her to dance to prove, well, something. Now he wasn't sure what. Three nights ago, he'd been attracted by her looks. Intrigued by her wit. Drawn by her touch. Frankly, she was right. The way he felt this minute wasn't a whole lot different from that.

However, Grace Munroe had made her wishes known. On a less primal level, he agreed. At the edge of the dance floor, he released her and stepped away.

"I'll let you get back to your party."

A look—was it respect?—faded up in her eyes. "Say hi to Teagan and your brothers for me."

"Will do."

Although these days the siblings rarely saw each other. But Cole was set to tie the knot soon with Australian television producer Taryn Quinn, which meant a family gathering complete with wily stepmother, stalked father and, inevitably, questions surrounding the altered state of Wynn's own personal life.

Until recently, he—not Cole or Dex—had been the brother destined for marriage. Of course, that was before the former love of his life, Heather Matthews, had informed the world that actually, she'd made other plans. When the bomb had hit, he'd slogged through the devastated stage, the angry phase. Now, he was comfortable just cruising along. So comfortable, in fact, he had no desire to ever lay open his heart to anyone again for any reason, sexy Grace Munroe included.

Wynn found the bride and groom, did the right thing and wished them nothing but happiness. On his way out of the room, which was thumping with music now, he bumped into Brock again. Wynn had a feeling it wasn't by accident.

"I see you shared a dance with my daughter," Brock said.

"For old time's sake."

"She might have told you…Grace left New York twelve months ago. She's staying on in Manhattan for a few days, getting together with friends." He mentioned the name of the prestigious hotel. "If you wanted to call in, see how she's doing… Well, I'd appreciate it. Might help keep some bad memories at bay." Brock lowered his voice. "She lost someone close to her recently."

"She mentioned her grandfather—"

"This was a person around her age." The older man's mouth twisted. "He was a firefighter. A good man. They were set to announce their engagement before the accident."

The floor tilted beneath Wynn's feet. Concentrating, he rubbed his temple—that scar.

"Grace was engaged?"

"As good as. The accident happened a year ago last week here in New York."

Wynn had believed Grace when she'd said that their night was a one-off—that she'd never gone home with a man before on a whim. Now the pieces fit. On that unfortunate anniversary, Grace had drowned out those memories by losing herself in Wynn's company. He wasn't upset by her actions; he understood them better than most. Hadn't he found solace—oblivion—in someone else's arms, too?

"She puts on a brave face." Brock threw a weary glance around the room. "But being here at one of her best friends' weddings, in front of so many others who know... She should have been married herself by now." Brock squared his heavy shoulders. "No one likes to be pitied. No one wants to be alone."

Brock wished Wynn the best with his make-believe meeting in the morning. Wynn was almost at the door when the music stopped and the DJ announced, "Calling all eligible ladies. Gather round. The bride is ready to throw her bouquet!"

Wynn cast a final glance back. He was interested to see that Grace hadn't positioned herself for the toss; she stood apart and well back from the rest.

A drumroll echoed out through the sound system. In her fluffy white gown, the beaming bride spun around. With an arm that belonged in the majors, she lobbed the weighty bunch well over her head. A collective gasp went up as the bouquet hurtled through the air, high over the outstretched arms of the nearest hopefuls. Over outliers' arms, as well. It kept flying and flying.

Straight toward Grace.

As the bouquet dropped from the ceiling, Grace realized at the last moment that she was in the direct line of fire. Rather than catch it, however, she stepped aside and petals smacked the polished floor near her feet. Then, as if wrenched by an invisible cord, the bouquet continued to slide. It stopped dead an inch from Wynn's shoes. The room stilled before all eyes shot from the flowers to Grace.

The romantically minded might have seen this curious event as an omen. Might have thought that the trajectory of the bouquet as it slid along the floor from Grace to Wynn meant they ought to get together. Only most guests here would know. Grace didn't want a fiancé.

She was still grieving the one she had lost.

As he and Grace stared at each other, anticipation vibrated off the walls and Wynn felt a stubborn something creak deep inside him. An awareness that had lain frozen and unfeeling these past months thawed a degree, and then a single icicle snapped and fell away from his soul.

Hunkering down, he collected the flowers. With their audience hushed and waiting, he headed back to Grace.

When he stopped less than an arm's distance away, he inspected the flowers—red and white roses with iridescent fern in between. But he didn't hand over the bouquet. Rather, he circled his arm around Grace's back and, in front of the spellbound crowd, slowly—deliberately—lowered his head over hers.

Two

As he drew her near, two things flashed through Grace's mind.

What in God's name is Wynn Hunter doing?

The other thought evaporated into a deep, drugging haze when the remembered heat of his mouth captured hers. At the same instant her limbs turned to rubber, her fingertips automatically wound into his lapels. Her toes curled and her core contracted, squeezing around a kernel of mindless want.

This man's kiss was spun from dreams. The hot, strong feel of him, the taste…his scent…

From the time she'd left his suite that night, she had wondered. The hours she'd spent in his bed had seemed so magical, perhaps she'd only dreamed them up. But this moment was real, and now she only wanted to experience it all again—his lips drifting over her breasts, his hands stroking, hips rocking.

When his lips gradually left hers, the burning feel of

him remained. With her eyes closed, she focused on the hard press of his chest against her bodice…her need to have him kiss her again. Then, from the depths of her kiss-induced fog, Grace heard a collective sigh go up in the room. With her head still whirling, she dragged open heavy eyes. Wynn's face was slanted over hers. He was smiling softly.

In a matter of seconds, he had made her forget about everything other than this. But the encounter three nights ago had been a mutually agreed upon, ultraprivate affair. This scene had been played out in front of an audience. Friends, and friends of friends, who knew what had happened last year.

Or thought that they knew.

Grace kept her unsteady voice hushed. "What are you doing?"

"Saying goodbye properly." With his arm still a strong band around her, he took a step back. "Are you all right to stand?"

She shook off more of her stupor. "Of course I can stand." But as she moved to disengage herself, she almost teetered.

With a knowing grin, he handed over the bouquet, which she mechanically accepted at the same time the DJ's voice boomed through the speakers.

"How about that, folks! What do you say? Is that our next bride-to-be?"

The applause was hesitant at first before the show of support went through the roof. Grace cringed at the attention. On another level, it also gave a measure of relief. Anything—including a huge misunderstanding—was better than the sea of pitying faces she'd had to endure that day.

"If you want," Wynn murmured, "I can stay longer."

With her free hand, she smoothed down her skirt—

and gathered the rest of her wits. "I'm sure you've done enough."

His gaze filtered over her face, lingering on her lips, still moist and buzzing from his kiss. Then, looking as hot as any Hollywood hunk, he turned and sauntered away.

A heartbeat later, the lights faded, music blared again and Amy Calhoun caught ahold of Grace's hand. As Amy dragged her to a relatively quiet corner, out of general view, her red ringlets looked set to combust with excitement.

"Who was *that*?" she cried.

Still lightheaded, Grace leaned back against the wall. "You don't want to know."

"I saw you two dancing. Did you only meet tonight? I mean, you don't have to say a word. I'm just curious, like friends are." Amy squeezed Grace's hand. "It's so good to see you happy."

"I look happy?" She felt spacey. Agitated.

In need of a cold shower.

"If you want to know, you look swept off your feet." The plump lips covering Amy's overbite twitched. "I actually thought that's what he'd do. Lift you up into his arms and carry you away."

Amy was an only child. She and Grace had grown up tight, spending practically every weekend at each other's places on Long Island—dressing up as princesses, enjoying the latest Disney films. Amy still lived and espoused a Cinderella mentality; a happily-ever-after would surely come if only a girl believed. An optimistic mindset was never a bad thing. However, with regard to this situation, Amy's sentimental nature was a bust.

"Wynn and I had met before tonight. It happened." Grace tossed the flowers aside on a table. "It's over."

"Okay." Amy's pearl chocker bobbed as she swallowed. "So, when you say *it* happened, you mean *it* as in…"

"As in intercourse. One night of amazing, mind-blowing, unforgettable sex." Grace groaned out a breath. God, it felt good to get that off her chest.

"Wow." Amy held her brow as if her head might be spinning. "Mind-blowing, huh? That's great. *Fantastic*. I'm just a little—"

"Shocked?"

"In a good way," Amy gave her a sympathetic look. "We've all been so worried."

As that familiar sick feeling welled up inside her, Grace flinched. "No one needs to be."

"I'm sure everyone knows that now. Sam was a great guy…a decorated firefighter from an awesome family. We all loved him. And he loved you—so much. But you needed something to push you to move on."

Those last words pulled Grace up.

But Wynn's invitation to this wedding was based on a lapsed friendship with the groom. He wasn't in the loop, and it was a stretch to think that someone had mentioned a bridesmaid's tragic personal situation over coffee and wedding cake.

Unless her father had said something.

Except the bouquet sliding from her feet across to his had been pure fluke. If not for that, he would never have had the opportunity to… How had he put it? Say goodbye properly. No way had he kissed her to simply show them all that she wasn't as fragile and alone as they might think.

And Wynn certainly wouldn't have swooped in to play superhero if he'd had any inkling of what had transpired the night of that accident a year ago. But the truth had to come out sometime. She only needed to find the right time.

Puzzle it out the right way.

Three days later, as his workday drew to a close, Wynn answered a conference call from his brothers on Skype.

"Bad time?"

Wynn smiled at Dex's laid-back expression and smooth voice. He was the epitome of a Hollywood producer ever since he'd taken over the family's movie unit in L.A.

"I have an easy four o'clock then I'm out of here," Wynn said.

"Off early, mate."

Skyping in from Sydney, Cole looked particularly tan after his sojourn with his fiancée Taryn Quinn on their yacht in the Pacific.

"Good to hear, bro," Dex said. "We all need time to chill."

"How's Dad?" Standing behind his chair, Wynn slipped one arm then the other into his jacket sleeves. That interview with Christopher Riggs—a job interview, and likely placement, based on a recommendation from Wynn's father—shouldn't take long. He'd get ready now to zip out the door as soon as he was done.

"No more attempts on his life since we spoke last," Cole replied, "and thank God for that."

"He's wondering if Tate should come home," Dex said.

"But Brandon thinks it's best to keep him out of harm's way," Cole explained, "at least until he can chase up some leads on that van."

Months back, during the stalker's last attack, Tate had almost been abducted along with his dad. Until the situation was sorted out and guilty parties thrown behind bars, the family had decided to place the youngest Hunter in a safer environment. Tate had spent time with the sweetheart/renegade of the family, Teagan, who lived in Seattle. And right now he was bunking down in Los Angeles with Dex. Tate had been happy with his movie-boss brother, and Dex had been happy with the boy's babysitter, Shelby Scott—in fact, she had recently become Dex's fiancée.

But now that there were leads on the van that had been

involved in that last assault, they might have a break in the case. Tate might soon be able to go home. Excellent.

"Brandon pinned down some snaps taken by a speed camera," Cole went on, "the same day Dad was attacked."

"Don't tell me after all this time he discovered the license plates were legit?" That they'd tracked down the assailant as easily as through a registration number.

Dex groaned. "Unfortunately, this creep isn't that stupid."

"But the traffic shots show the driver pulled over with a flat," Cole added.

"You have a description?" Wynn asked.

"Dark glasses, fake beard," Cole said. "Other than general height and weight, no help. But Brandon did a thorough survey of the area. A woman walking her Pomeranian remembers the van *and* the man. She also recalls him dropping his keys."

Dex took over. "She scooped them up. Before handing them back, she took note of the rental tag."

Leaning toward the screen, Wynn set both palms flat on the desk. "Weren't all the rental companies checked out?"

"The company concerned is a fly-by-nighter from another state," Dex explained.

"Brandon found the guy who ran it," Cole added. "Other than simply hiring out the car, he doesn't appear to be involved. But getting corresponding records was like pulling teeth."

"Until Brandon threatened to bring in the authorities, criminal as well as tax," Dex said. "The guy's got until tomorrow to cough up."

"Great work. So, Tate's staying with you in the meantime, Dex?"

"He and Shelby are as thick as thieves. He loves her cooking. I do, too. You should taste her cupcakes." Sitting back, ex-playboy Dex rested his hands on his stomach and licked his chops. "We're looking at taking the plunge some-time in the New Year. The wedding will most likely be in Mountain Ridge, Oklahoma, her hometown."

"Oh, I can see you now, riding up to the minister on matching steeds like something out of a '40s Western."

Wynn grinned at Cole's ribbing.

"Laugh if you dare," Dex said. "I bought a property that used to belong to Shelby's dad." Dex's tawny-colored gaze grew reflective. "One day we might settle out there for good."

"Away from the hype and glitter of Hollywood?" Wynn found that hard to believe.

"If it means being with Shelby," Dex assured them both, "I'd live in a tar shack."

Wynn was pleased for both brothers' happiness, even if he no longer possessed a romantic thought or inclina-tion in his body.

Barring the other night.

He felt for Grace and her situation. Covert glances and well-intentioned pity over past relationships that hadn't ended well... Painful to endure. Far better to give people something to really talk about. And so, with the entire room's eyes upon them, he'd kissed her—no half measures. After the shock had cleared, however, she'd looked ready to slap his face rather than thank him. It was a shame, be-cause after another taste of Grace Munroe's lips, he'd only wanted more.

Remembering that interview with Riggs, Wynn checked the time. "Guys, I need to sign off. Dad rang a couple of weeks back about giving a guy a job. Background in pub-lishing. Apparently great credentials and, quote, 'a finger on the pulse of solutions for challenges in this digital age.' Dad thought I could use him."

"Sounds great," Dex said. "Should help take some pres-sure off."

Wynn frowned. "I'm not under pressure." Or wouldn't be half so much when the merger deal he'd been working on was in the bag. For now, however, that arrangement was tightly under wraps—he hadn't even told his father about the merger plans.

"Well, it'll be strictly fun and games when you guys come out for the wedding." Pride shone from Cole's face. "You and Dex are my best men."

Wynn straightened. That was the first he'd heard of it. "I'm honored." Then his thoughts doubled back. "Can a groom have two best men?"

"It's the 21st century." Dex laughed. "You can do any damn thing you want."

"So, Wynn," Cole went on, "you're definitely coming?"

Dex's voice lowered. "You're okay after that breakup now, right?"

Wynn wanted to roll his eyes. He'd really hoped he'd get through this conversation without anyone bringing that up.

"*The breakup…*" He forced a grin. "Sounds like the title of some soppy book."

"Movie, actually," Dex countered.

"Well, you'll all be relieved to know that I've moved on."

"Mentally or physically?" Dex asked.

"Both."

"Really?" Cole said at the same time Dex asked, "Anyone we know?"

"As a matter of fact…remember Grace Munroe?"

Cole blinked twice. "You don't mean Brock Munroe's girl?"

"*Whoa.* I remember," Dex said. "The little horror who crushed on you that Christmas in Colorado when we were all kids."

"That's back to front." Wynn set them straight. "I wanted to crush her—under my heel."

"And now?" Dex asked.

"We caught up."

"So, we can put her name down beside yours for the wedding?" Cole prodded.

"I said I've moved on." Lifting his chin, Wynn adjusted his tie's Windsor knot. "No one's moving in."

In the past, these two had nudged each other, grinning over Wynn's plans to settle down sooner rather than later. Now Cole and Dex were the ones jabbed by Cupid's arrow and falling over themselves to commit while Wynn had welcomed the role of dedicated bachelor. Once bit and twice shy. He didn't need the aggravation.

The men signed off. Wynn could see his personal assistant Daphne Cranks down the hall trying to get his attention. She pushed her large-framed glasses up her nose before flicking her gaze toward a guest. A man dressed in an impeccable dark gray suit got up from his chair with an easy smile. Christopher Riggs was almost as tall as Wynn. He had a barrel chest like a buff character from a comic strip. When Wynn joined him, they shook hands, introduced themselves and headed for the boardroom.

"My father seems impressed by your credentials," Wynn said, pulling in his chair.

"He's a fascinating man."

"He worked hard to build Hunter Enterprises into the force it is today."

"I believe it was very much a local Australian concern when Guthrie took over from your grandfather."

"My father ran the company with my uncle for a short while. Two strong wills. Different ideas of how the place ought to run. I'm afraid it didn't work out." Wynn unbuttoned his jacket and sat back. "That was decades ago."

"Hopefully I'll have the chance to contribute something positive moving forward."

They discussed where the company was positioned at the moment, and went on to speak about publishing in general.

Christopher handed over his résumé and then volunteered information about his background. Guthrie had already mentioned that, until recently, Christopher's family had owned a notable magazine in Australia. Like so many businesses, the magazine had suffered in these harsh economic times. The Riggses had found a business partner who had buoyed the cash flow for a time before pulling the plug. The magazine had gone into receivership.

Christopher had a degree, a background in reporting and good references in marketing. Alongside that, he could talk rings around Wynn with regard to web presence statistics and methods, as well as social media strategies aimed at optimizing potential market share.

While they spoke, Wynn tried to look beyond the smooth exterior, deep into the man's clear mint-green eyes. No bad vibes. Christopher Riggs was the epitome of a composed professional. Even in his later years, Guthrie Hunter possessed an uncanny ability to sniff out true talent. Wynn could see Christopher well-placed in his marketing and tech team.

They discussed and then agreed on remuneration and benefits.

"Come in tomorrow." Wynn pushed to his feet. "Daphne can set you up in an office."

The men shook again and, with a bounce in his step, Christopher Riggs headed out.

After collecting his briefcase, Wynn came back into his private reception area. When he said good-night, Daphne held him up.

"These tickets arrived a few minutes ago." She gave him an embossed envelope. "A gift from the producer."

He was about to say that he wasn't interested in Broadway tonight—she was welcome to the tickets—but then he reconsidered.

Daphne was the most efficient personal assistant he'd

ever had. Always on top of things, constantly on his heels…
a bit of a puppy, he'd sometimes thought. Behind the Mr.
Magoo glasses and dull hairdo, she was probably attractive; however, from what he could gather, she was very
much single. He wasn't certain she even had friends. If he
left those tickets behind, chances were they'd be dropped
in the trash when five o'clock rolled around.

So he took the envelope as his thoughts swung to another
woman who was his assistant's opposite in every sense of
the word—except for the being single part.

Brock had mentioned Grace was in town for a few days.
Her hotel was around the corner. As he entered the elevator,
Wynn thought it over. Perhaps Grace had left New York by
now. And hadn't she made herself clear? She didn't regret
that night spent in his bed but she wasn't after an encore.
Grace didn't want to see him again.

As he slid the envelope into his inside breast pocket and
the elevator doors closed, Wynn hesitated, and then, remembering their last kiss, slowly grinned.

What the hell. He had nothing on tonight. Maybe he
could change her mind.

Three

Exiting the hotel elevator, Grace headed across the foyer and then pulled up with a start. Cutting a dynamite figure in a dark, tailored suit, Wynn Hunter stood at the reception counter, waiting to speak with someone behind the desk.

No need to assume he'd come to see her. There were a thousand other reasons he might be here tonight. Business. Friends. Another woman. An attractive, successful, single male like Wynn… Members of the opposite sex would flock to spend time with him.

She'd been on her way out to mull over a decision—whether or not to spend more time in New York before getting back to her job. Late last year she'd left New York to join a private practice in Florida as a speech-language pathologist. Providing tools to help both adults and children with communication disabilities was rewarding work. Just the other week, she'd got an update from a young mom who had needed additional support and advice on feeding her baby who'd been born with a cleft palate. The woman had wanted to let Grace know that the baby's first surgery, which included ear tubes to help with fluid buildup, had been a great success.

Grace had made good friends in Florida, too. Had a nice apartment in a great neighborhood. But she missed so much about New York—minus the memories surrounding Sam and his accident, of course, which seemed to pop up everywhere, constantly.

Except during that time she'd spent with Wynn.

Her lips still hummed and her body sang whenever she thought of the way they had kissed. She wasn't certain that, if she strolled over and started up a conversation with him now, one thing wouldn't lead to another. However, while the sex would be better than great, she'd already decided that their one-night stand should be left in the past. She wasn't ready to invite a man, and associated complications, into her life.

Best just to keep going without saying hi.

He seemed to wait until she was out in the open before rapping his knuckles on the counter and then absently turning around. In that instant, she felt his focus narrow and lock her in its sights. No choice now. She pulled up again.

He crossed over to her at a leisurely pace. People in his path naturally made way for him. In the three days since they'd spoken last, his raven's-wing hair had grown enough to lick his collar. The shadow on his jaw looked rougher, too. And his eyes seemed even darker—their message more tempting.

She remembered his raspy cheek grazing her flesh… the magic of his mouth on her thigh…his muscular frame bearing down again and again to meet her hips. And then he was standing in front of her and speaking in that deep, dreamy voice.

"You're on your way out?"

Willing her thumping heartbeat to slow, Grace nodded. "And you? Here on business?"

"Your father mentioned you were staying here for a few days." He waved an envelope. "I have tickets for a show. We could catch a bite first."

He was here to see her?

"Wynn, I'd really like to, but—"

"You have another date?"

She shook her head.

"You've already eaten?"

No, but suddenly she could taste the rich fudge ice-cream they'd devoured, eating off the same spoon that night when they had both needed to cool down.

Grace pushed the image aside. "I'm sorry. This doesn't work for me."

"Because it's not a good time."

For a relationship of any kind. She nodded. "That's right."

He seemed to weigh that up before asking, "When are you leaving New York?"

"I'm not sure. Soon."

"So, worst case scenario—we have a dog-awful time tonight and you won't need to bump into me again for another twenty years."

It sounded so harmless. And maybe it was.

Brock Munroe was a devoted father to all three of his daughters. He'd always been there, watching out for their best interests—doing what he could to help. Did that include organizing some male company to help divert her from unpleasant memories while she was back in town?

And if her father had gone so far as to suggest this get-together, what else had Wynn and her dad discussed? Had Sam been mentioned at all? To what extent? If Wynn had spoken with her mother, the subject of her past boyfriend would definitely have come up. Suzanne Munroe had thought of Sam as a son—always would—and she took every opportunity to let others know it.

There'll never be another Sam.

"Wynn, did my father put you up to this?" she asked.

Wynn's chin kicked up a notch. "Brock did mention it might be nice for us to catch up again while you were in town."

Grace sighed.

"I like to think of my father's smile if he found out his plan here had worked, but—"

"Grace, I'm not here because your father suggested it."

"It's okay. Honest. I—"

He laughed. "Come on now. I'm here because I want to be." When she hesitated, he went on. "We don't have to go to the show. But you have to eat. I know a great place on Forty-second."

She paused. "What place?"

He named a restaurant that she knew and loved.

"Great food," he added.

She agreed. "I remember."

"Their chocolate *panna cotta* is sensational."

"The mushroom risotto, too."

Wincing, he held his stomach. "Personally, I'm starved. I skipped lunch."

"I grabbed an apple-pie melt off a truck."

"I love apple-pie melts."

When he sent her a slanted smile, her heart gave a kick and, next thing she knew, she was nodding.

"All right," she said.

"So, that's a yes? To dinner, or dinner and the show? It's an opening night musical. The scores are supposed to be amazing."

Then he mentioned the name of the lead actor. Who said no to that? Only she wasn't exactly dressed for the theater.

"I need to go up and change first," she said.

But then, his gaze sharpened—almost gleamed—and Grace took stock again. Was he debating whether or not to suggest a drink in her room before heading out? Given the conflagration the last time they'd been alone together, no matter how great the songs or the food, she guessed he wouldn't complain if they ordered room service and bunked down in her bedroom for the night.

She was reconsidering the whole deal when his expression cleared and he waved the envelope toward a lounge adjoining the lobby.

"I'll wait over there," he said. "Take your time."

As he headed off, Grace blinked and then eased into a smile. No inviting himself up or flirty innuendoes. Perfect. Except…

If Wynn wasn't here at her father's behest, or to test the air for some no-strings-attached sex, that made tonight about a mutually attracted couple who wanted to enjoy some time together. In other words, a date.

Her first in a year.

"Some like it steamy." As he walked alongside her, Wynn gave her a puzzled look. Grace indicated a billboard across the street. "There," she explained. "It's the name of a new movie."

Wynn grinned. "Sounds like something my brother would dream up."

She and Wynn were heading back to the hotel. They'd enjoyed their meal and the show had been fantastic.

During dinner, she'd caught up on all the Hunter news. Apparently Cole and Dex had been at loggerheads for years. When their father had decided to split the company among the kids, workaholic Cole had expected more from Dex than he'd thought Mr. Casual could give. Dex had been happy to get away on his own to California to head Hunter Productions, which, after some challenges, was now doing well.

Teagan had got out of the family business altogether. She'd followed brother Dex to the States and had forged a successful health and fitness business in Seattle. Grace decided she really ought to get in touch with her old friend again.

As for the show, the staging had been spectacular and singing amazing; more than once, Grace had had to swallow past the lump in her throat. And Wynn's company had been as intoxicating as ever. Despite her reservations, she was glad he'd convinced her to go out.

"I know Cole's getting married," she said as her attention shifted from the billboard to take in Wynn's classic profile. "But isn't Dex engaged, too? I'm sure I saw an announcement somewhere."

"I get to meet both Dex's and Cole's love interests in a couple of weeks. Cole's wedding's back home in Sydney."

In Australia? She remembered wondering about his accent that first night; she'd thought possibly English but hadn't wanted to get into backgrounds. "A Hunter wedding. Set to be the social event of the season, I bet."

Grunting, he flipped his jacket's hem back to slot both hands in his pockets. "I wouldn't count on that."

The Hunters were wealthy, well connected. When Guthrie had remarried a few years ago, her parents had attended. Grace's mother had come home gushing over the extravagance of the reception as well as the invitation list—sporting legends, business magnates, some of the biggest names in Hollywood today. But it sounded as if Cole and his bride-to-be might be planning a more private affair.

Grace was about to ask more when a raindrop landed on her nose. She checked out the sky. A second and third raindrop smacked her forehead and her chin. Then the starless sky seemed to split wide apart.

As the deluge hit, Grace yelped. Wynn caught her hand, hauling her out of the downpour and into the cozy alcove of a handy shopfront.

"It'll pass soon," he said with an authoritative voice that sounded as if he could command the weather rather than predict it.

With his hair dripping and features cast in soft-edged shadows, he looked so assured. So handsome. Was it possible for a man to be *too* masculine? Too take-me-now sexy?

As he flicked water from his hands, his focus shifted from the rain onto her. As if he'd read her thoughts, his gaze searched hers before he carefully reached for her cheek. But he only swept away the wet hair that was plastered over her nose, around her chin.

"Are you cold?" he asked.

She thought for a moment then feigned a shiver and nodded.

He maneuvered her to stand with her back to him. He held open his silk-lined, wool-blend jacket and cocooned her against a wall of muscle and heat. *Heavenly.* Then his strong arms folded across her and tugged her in super close.

Surrendering, Grace let her eyes drift shut. She might not want to get involved, but she was human and, damn, this felt good.

His stubble grazed her temple. "Warm now?"

Grinning, she wiggled back against him. "Not yet."

When his palms flattened against her belly, slowly ironing up before skimming back down, she bit her lip to contain the sigh. Then his hug tightened at the same time his fingers fanned and gradually spread lower. She let her head rock back and rest against his shoulder.

"Better?" he asked against her ear.

"Not yet," she lied.

"If we keep it up," he murmured, "we might need to explain ourselves to the police in that patrol car over there."

"We're not exactly causing a scene."

"Not yet."

He nuzzled down beneath her scarf and dropped a lingering kiss on the side of her throat as one hand coasted higher, over her ribs, coming to rest beneath the slope of her breast. When his thumb brushed her nipple, back and forth three times, she quivered all over.

She felt his chest expand before he turned her around. In the shadows, she caught a certain glimmer in his eyes. Then his gaze zeroed in on her mouth as his grip tightened on her shoulders.

"Grace, precisely how much do you want to heat up?"

Her heartbeat began to race. No denying—they shared a chemistry, a connection, like two magnets meant to lock whenever they crossed paths. She'd had fun this evening. She knew he had, too. And the way he was looking at her now—as if he could eat her...

On a purely primal level, she wanted the flames turned up to high. But if she weakened and slept with Wynn again tonight, how would she feel about herself in the morning? Perhaps simply satisfied. Or would she wish that she'd remembered her earlier stand?

She liked Wynn. She adored the delicious way he made her feel. Still, it was best to put on the brakes.

Sometimes when she thought about Sam, the years they'd spent together, the night that he had died—it all seemed like a lifetime ago and yet still so "now." Before she could truly move forward and think about starting something new, she needed to make sense of what had come before.

The loss.

Her guilt.

Lowering her gaze, Grace turned to face the street. The display featured in the shop window next to them caught her eye. They were sheltering from the rain in a bookshop doorway. The perfect in for a change of subject.

"Does Hunter Publishing own bookstores?" she asked.

Wynn combed long fingers back through his hair then

shook out the moisture as if trying to shake off his steamier thoughts.

"We handle magazines and newspapers," he told her, "not novels."

"Everyone's supposed to have at least one story in them," she murmured, thinking aloud.

She certainly had one. Nothing she wanted professionally published, of course. But she knew that committing unresolved feelings to paper could be therapeutic.

"Have you got a flight booked back home?" he asked as the rain continued to fall.

"Actually I was thinking of taking a little more time off."

Hands in his pockets, Wynn leaned back against the shop door. "How much time?"

"A couple of weeks." Another experienced therapist had just started with the practice. Grace's boss had said, although she was relatively new, if she needed a bit more time off, it shouldn't be a problem.

His eyes narrowed as he gave her a cryptic grin. "You should come to Cole's wedding with me."

She blinked twice. "You're not serious."

"I am serious."

"You want me to jump on a plane and travel halfway around the world with you, just like that?" She pulled a face. "That's crazy."

"Not crazy. You know all the old crowd. I already told my brothers that we caught up."

Her heart skipped a beat. Exactly how much had he told them? "What did they say?" she asked.

"They said you had a crush on me when you were six."

"When you were such a dweeb?"

"I was focused."

She teased, "Focused, but clumsy."

She could attest to the fact that he'd outgrown the clumsy phase.

"Cole suggested it earlier today. I brushed it off, but after tonight…" He pushed off from the door and stood up straight. "It'll be fun."

The idea of catching up with his family was certainly tempting. After that Christmas, she and Teagan had been pen pals for a long while. Then Tea had that accident and was in and out of hospital with a string of surgeries. Tea's letters had dwindled to the point where they'd finally lost touch.

But foremost a trip to Australia would mean spending loads of time with Wynn, which didn't add up to slowing things down or giving herself the time she still needed to work through and accept her past with Sam.

She waved the suggestion off. "You don't need me."

"That's right. I *want* you."

Such a simple yet complicated statement—it took her aback.

She tried to make light. "You must have a mile-long list of women to choose from."

His brows knitted. "You have that wrong. Dex was the playboy. Never me."

When a group of boisterous women walked by the alcove, he stepped forward to gauge the prewinter night sky.

"Rain's stopped," he said. "Let's go before we get caught again."

As they walked side by side past puddles shimmering with light from the neon signs and streetlamps, Wynn thought back.

By age ten, he'd had a handle on the concept of delayed gratification. If he needed the blue ribbon in swim squad, he put in time at the pool. If he wanted to win his father's approval, he studied until he excelled. Reward for effort was the motto upon which he'd built his life, professional as well as private.

Then Heather had walked away and that particular view on life had changed.

On the night he and Grace had met again, Wynn had seen what he'd wanted and decided simply to take it. A few minutes ago, with her bundled against him in those shadows, the same thousand-volt arc had crackled between them. For however long it lasted, he wanted to enjoy it. More than gut said Grace wanted that, too, even if she seemed conflicted.

Hell, if she had time off, why not come to Australia? He could show her some sights. They could share a few laughs. No one needed to get all heavy and "forever" about it. He wasn't out to replace her ex. He understood certain scars didn't heal.

Maybe it would make a difference if he let her know that.

"Should we have a nightcap?" he asked as they entered the relative quiet of her hotel lobby a few minutes later. "I found a nice spot in that lounge earlier. No piano though."

She continued on, heading for the elevators. "I have to get up early."

When she didn't elaborate, Wynn adjusted his plan. He'd say his piece when he said good-night at her door. At the elevators, however, she cut down that idea, too.

"It's been a great night," she said, after he'd hit the Up key. "But I think I'll say good-night here."

He was forming words to reply when he heard a woman's laugh—throaty, familiar. All the muscles in his stomach clenched tight a second before he tracked down the source. Engaged in conversation with a jet-set rock'n'roll type, Heather Matthews was strolling across a nearby stretch of marble tiles.

Wynn's heart dropped.

Over eight million people and New York could still be a freaking small world.

At the same time his ex glanced in his direction, the elevator pinged and the doors slid open. He shepherded Grace inside and stabbed a button. As the doors closed, the ice in his blood began to thaw and the space between collar and neck started to steam. It took a moment before he realized Grace was studying him.

"Inviting yourself up?" she drawled.

"I'll say good-night at the door."

"Because of that woman you want to avoid?" She hit a floor key. "Want to tell me who she is?"

His jaw clenched. "Not particularly."

She didn't probe, which he appreciated. Except, maybe it would help if Grace knew that he'd recently lost someone, too, though in a different way.

He tugged at his tie, loosening the knot that was pressing on his throat. "That woman and I...we were together for a few years. There was a time I thought we'd get married," he added. "Have a family. She didn't see it that way."

Her eyes rounded then filled with sympathy. The kind of pity Wynn abhorred and, he thought, Grace knew well.

"Wynn...I'm sorry."

"It's in the past." Drawing himself up to his full height, he shrugged. "I'm happy for Cole. For Dex, too. But I'm steering clear of that kind of—" heartache? "—commitment."

A bell pinged and the elevator doors opened. She stepped out, and then, with a look, let him know he could follow. She stopped outside a door midway down the corridor, flipped her key card over the sensor. When the light blinked on, she clicked open the door and, after an uncertain moment, faced him again. They were both damp from the rain. Drops still glistened in her hair.

"For what it's worth," she said, "I think your ex missed out."

Then she stepped forward and craned up on her toes. When her lips brushed his cheek, time seemed to wind down. She lingered there. If she was going to step away, she wasn't in too much of a hurry. She had to get up early. Had wanted to say good-night. But if he wasn't mistaken, this was his cue.

His hands cupped her shoulders. As her face angled up, his head dropped down. When his mouth claimed hers, he held off a beat before winding one arm around her back. He felt more than heard the whimper in her throat. A heartbeat later, she relaxed and then melted.

As his tongue pushed past her lips, a thick molten stream coursed through his veins. The delicious surge…that visceral tug… And then her arms coiled around his neck and the connection started to sizzle.

He hadn't planned on taking Grace to bed tonight. He knew she hadn't planned this, either. But what could he say? Plans changed.

A muttering at his back seeped through the fog.

"For pity's sake, get a room."

Grace stiffened, and then pried herself away. Down the hall, a middle-aged couple were shaking their heads as they disappeared into a neighboring suite. Coming close again, Wynn slid a hand down her side.

Get a room.

"Maybe that's not such a bad idea," he murmured against her brow.

When she didn't respond, he drew back. A pulse was popping in her throat, but reason had returned to her eyes.

"Good night, Wynn."

"What about Sydney?"

"I'll let you know."

"Soon." He handed over a business card with his numbers.

Before her soft smile disappeared behind the crack in the door, she agreed. "Yes, Wynn. Soon."

Four

The next morning, Wynn arrived at the office early.

By seven, he was downstairs, speaking with his editor-in-chief about a plagiarism claim that was causing the legal department major grief. An hour and a half later, he was heading back upstairs and thinking about Grace. They had parted amicably, to say the least. He thought there was a chance she might even take him up on the invitation to accompany him to Cole's wedding.

He'd give her a day, and then try her at the hotel. Or he could get her cell number from Brock. Even if she decided not to go to Sydney, he wanted to take her out again. By the time he got back to the States, she would have left New York and gone back to her life in Florida.

Wynn made his way past Daphne's vacant desk; his assistant was running a little late. A moment later, when he swung open his office door, he was called back—but not by Daphne. Christopher Riggs was striding up behind him, looking as enthusiastic as he had the previous day at his interview.

"Hey, Wynn." Christopher ran a hand through his hair, pushing a dark wave off his brow. "Daphne wasn't at her desk. I thought I'd take a chance and see if you were in."

Wynn flicked a glance at his watch. His next meeting—an important one—wasn't far off. But he could spare a few minutes.

As they moved inside his office, Christopher's expression sharpened when something on Wynn's desk caught his eye—the interconnecting silver L and T of a publishing logo. "La Trobes," he said.

Leaning back against the edge of the desk, Wynn crossed his arms. "Impress me with your knowledge."

"I know La Trobes's publications have a respectable share of the marketplace."

"Keeping in mind that print share is shrinking."

"But there are other, even greater opportunities outside of print, if they're harnessed properly. I've given a lot of thought to out-of-the-box strategies and the implementation of facilities for digital readers to be compatible with innovative applications."

For the next few minutes, Wynn listened to an extended analysis of the digital marketplace. Obviously this guy knew his stuff. But now wasn't the time to get into a full-blown discussion.

After a few more minutes of Christopher sharing his ideas, Wynn got up from the desk and interrupted. "I have a meeting. We'll talk later."

A muscle in Christopher's jaw jumped twice. He was pumped, ready to let loose with a thousand initiatives. But he quickly reined himself in.

"Of course," he said, backing up. "I'll get out of your hair."

Christopher was headed out when Daphne appeared at the open door.

"Oh, sorry to interrupt," Daphne said. "I didn't realize—"

As she backed up, her elbow smacked the jamb. When her trusty gold-plated pen jumped from her hand, Christopher swooped to rescue it. As he returned the pen, Wynn didn't miss the wink he sent its owner. He also noted Daphne's blush and her preoccupation as Christopher vacated the room.

Rousing herself, she nudged those glasses back up her nose and, in the navy blue dress reserved for Thursdays, moved forward. As Wynn dragged in his seat, Daphne lowered into her regular chair on the other side of his desk. So—head back in the game. First up, before that meeting, he needed to make some arrangements.

"I'm flying to Sydney Monday."

Daphne crossed her legs and scribbled on her pad. "Returning when?"

"Keep it open."

"I'll organize a car to the airport." She scrunched her pert nose. "Will you need accommodation?"

"We're all staying at the family home. Guthrie wants us all in one place leading up to the big day."

If Grace decided to join him, he'd make additional arrangements. Lots of them.

As Daphne took notes, her owlish, violet-blue eyes sparkled behind their lenses. He couldn't be sure, but he suspected his assistant was a romantic. She liked the thought of a wedding. Not so long ago, she had really liked Heather.

The two women had met several times. Daphne had commented on how carefree, beautiful and friendly his partner was. The morning after Heather had left him sitting alone in that restaurant, he'd returned to his apartment and had lain like a fallen redwood on his couch. He'd let his phone ring and ring. He didn't eat. Didn't drink. When an urgent knocking had forced him to his feet, he'd found Daphne standing, fretting in his doorway. Looking pale, she'd announced, "I've been calling all day." For the first time in their history, her tone had been heated. Concerned.

He had groaned out his story and had felt a little better for it. Afterward, she'd made coffee and a sandwich he couldn't taste. Then she'd simply sat alongside of him, keeping him company without prying or hassling about the meetings he'd missed. They hadn't spoken about that day since, but he wasn't sorry she'd appeared on his doorstep and had seen that shattered man. He trusted her without reservation. He knew she would always be there for him, as a top assistant, even as an unlikely friend.

Now, like every weekday, he and Daphne went through the day's schedule.

"Midmorning," Daphne said, "you have a meeting with digital strategists."

To make existing online sites more efficient and user-friendly while increasing cross-promotional links between Hunter Publishing's properties.

"At two, a consultation with the financial heads," she went on.

To get down to the pins and tacks of whether his proposed partial merger with another publisher—Episode Features—was as viable as he believed.

Daphne glanced at the polished-steel wall clock. "In a few minutes," she said, "a meeting with Paul Lumos."

Episode's CEO. They were both anxious to finalize outstanding sticking points. Neither man wanted leaks to either the public, employees or, in Wynn's case, his family.

Normally, walls didn't exist between Hunter father and son. This was an exception. During a recent phone conversation, Wynn had brought up the subject of mergers. Guthrie had cut the conversation down with a single statement. "Not interested." His father's business model was built around buyouts and takeovers. He didn't agree with handing over *any* controlling interest. Even in these challenging times, this giant oak would not bend. But with the regularity of print-run schedules cut in half, both Lumos and Wynn saw critical benefits in sharing overheads relating to factory and delivery costs.

As Brock Munroe had said: adapt or die.

Daphne was leaving the office when Wynn's private line announced an incoming call. His father. Sitting back, Wynn checked his watch. Lumos was due any moment. He'd need to make this brief.

"Checking in," Guthrie said. "Making sure we'll see you next week."

Smiling, Wynn sat back. "The flight's booked."

"I just got off the phone with Dex and Tate." His father pushed out a weary breath. "This place feels so empty without that boy's smile."

Wynn read his father's thoughts. *Did I do the right thing sending my youngest son away?* He'd had no choice.

"We all agreed. While there's any risk of Tate being caught up again in that trouble, it's best he stay somewhere safe."

It had also been agreed that *all* the Hunters should return home for Cole's wedding. Since that last incident, where father and child had very nearly been abducted, additional security had been arranged. On conference calls, the older Hunter brothers had discussed with Brandon Powell how to increase those measures these coming weeks.

"Any news on that car rental company's records?" Wynn asked.

"The license plate was a fake," Guthrie confirmed. "After hiring the van, the plates were switched and switched again before dropping it back. If that woman Brandon interviewed hadn't caught sight of the rental company's name on the keys, we'd be clueless. Now at least we have some kind of description of the man."

"Was a sketch artist brought in?"

"Should have something on that soon." Guthrie exhaled. "God help me, I want to know what's behind all this."

Wynn imagined his father standing by the giant arched window in the second-story master suite of his magnificent Sydney house—the estate that Wynn and his brothers had called home growing up. The frustration, the fury, must be eating him alive.

"We're getting closer, Dad." Hopefully soon his father would have his life back and Tate could go home to Sydney for good.

Wynn changed the subject.

"Christopher Riggs started today."

His father sounded sure-footed again. "That boy has good credentials. Christopher's father worked for me years ago. Later, he bought a low distribution magazine that he built up. A recent merger turned out to be a death sentence. The family's interests were swallowed up and spat out."

Wynn's stomach tightened. But his father couldn't know about his meetings with Lumos or his merger plans for Hunter Publishing.

"Christopher's father is a good friend," Guthrie continued. "Someone I would trust with my life. When Tobias and I had our falling out, it was Vincent Riggs I turned to. I wanted to fold—give my brother any damn thing he wanted if he agreed to stay and help run the company—it was our father's dying wish. But Vincent helped clear my head. Tobias and I did things differently. Thought differently. Still do. We would have ended up killing each other if he'd stayed on. I'll always be grateful to Vincent for making me see that. Giving his only son this opportunity is the least I can do."

Wynn was sitting back, rubbing the scar on his forehead

as he stared at the portrait of his father hanging on the wall. He couldn't imagine how betrayed Guthrie would feel when he found out he'd gone behind his back organizing that deal.

"You there, son?"

Wynn cleared his throat. "Yeah. Sorry. I have a meeting in five."

"I won't hold you up."

His father muttered a goodbye and Wynn pushed out of his chair. When his gaze found the La Trobes folder on his desk, he remembered Guthrie's words and his chest burned again. His father had spoken of how, in his dealings with Uncle Tobias, he'd needed to accept that sometimes the answer to a problem is: there is no answer.

And now, Wynn had no option, either. He had to pursue this merger deal. No matter the casualties or hard feelings—he needed to keep his corner of the Hunter empire strong.

Five

"Well, now, this is a surprise."

At the sound of Wynn's greeting and sight of his intrigued smile, the nerves in Grace's stomach knotted up. Wearing a white business shirt, which stretched nicely across his chest, a crimson tie and dark suit pants that fit his long, strong legs to perfection, he looked so incredibly tasty, her mouth wanted to water.

"I was out doing a few things," she replied as he crossed his large private reception area. "When I passed your building, I thought I might catch you before you left for the day."

When Grace had arrived, the assistant had let Wynn know he had a visitor. Now, as the young woman packed up for the day, pushing to her feet and securing a massive handbag over her shoulder, Grace noticed the interested—*or was that protective?*—glance she sent Wynn's way. Wearing serious glasses and a dress that had submitted to the press of an iron one too many times, the woman looked more suited to court dictation than boardroom infatuation. But wasn't it always the quiet ones?

A moment later, Grace was following Wynn into his spacious office suite.

To the left, black leather settees were arranged in a *U* formation around a low Perspex occasional table stacked with three neat piles of magazines and newspapers. A spotless fireplace was built into the oak-paneled wall. To one side of the mantle sat a framed copy of a well-known Hunter magazine—on the other hung an identically framed copy of the *New York Globe*, Hunter Publishing's primary newspaper; their offices were located on a lower floor. But what drew her attention most was the view of Midtown visible beyond those wall-to-wall windows. It never got old.

From this vantage point, gazing out over Times Square toward Rockefeller Center, she felt settled, warm—as if she were swaddled in a cashmere wrap.

She wandered over and set a palm against the cool glass. "I've missed this."

A few seconds later, Wynn's voice rumbled out from behind her.

"Growing up," he said, "I remember my father being away a lot. He had good people in key positions here in New York, but he wanted to keep an eagle eye on things himself. When he said he trusted me enough to take on that gatekeeping role, I almost fell out of my chair. I was twenty-three when I started my grooming here."

The deep, rich sound of his voice, the comfort of his body heat warming her back… She really needed to say her piece and get out of here before her knees got any weaker.

As she turned to face him, however, her blouse brushed his shirtfront and that weak-kneed feeling gripped her doubly tight. The message in his gaze wasn't difficult to read. She was a confident, intelligent woman who had her act together for the most part, yet she felt like a sieve full of warm putty whenever Wynn Hunter looked at her that way.

She moistened her lips. "I've decided not to go to Sydney."

His eyebrows knitted before his gaze dipped to her mouth, then combed over one cheek. She felt the appraisal like a touch.

"That's a shame." With a curious grin hooking one side of his mouth, he edged a little closer. "Sure I can't convince you?"

"If we arrive and stay there together... Well, I just don't want to give anyone the wrong idea."

"What idea is that? That we're a couple?"

"Yes, actually."

"And that would make you uncomfortable. Make you feel disloyal to your ex." He explained, "Your dad mentioned what happened last year. It must've been hard."

Her stomach began to churn in that sick way it did whenever someone said those words to her.

"I'm working through it," she told him, crossing to his desk and stopping to one side of the big, high-backed chair.

"No one has to know any background," he said.

"Your family will ask questions."

"Trust me." He followed her. "They'll only be jazzed about seeing you again. Particularly Teagan."

She exhaled. He never gave up. "Wynn, we've known each other five minutes." *This time.*

"I'd like to get to know you more."

When his fingertips feathered the back of her hand, she eased away around the other side of the chair. "I'm not ready for this."

"I'm talking about soaking up gobs of therapeutic, subtropical sunshine. Have you any idea how soft a koala's fur feels beneath your fingertips?"

She narrowed her eyes at him. "Not fair."

He moved around the chair to join her. When his fingers slipped around hers, she was infused with his heat.

She wanted to move away again. Tell him that he couldn't talk her around. Only these toasty feelings were getting harder to ignore. She could so easily give in to the urge, tip forward.

Let go.

"I lay awake last night," he said, moving closer. "I was thinking about our evening together. About putting the past in the past for a couple of weeks."

She remembered again how candidly he'd spoken about his ex. She'd seen it in the shadows of his eyes. He'd been badly hurt, too.

In some ways, he understood. And Grace understood him.

She couldn't fix it with Sam, but Wynn was here, in her present. He'd been nothing but thoughtful toward her. And he wasn't looking to set up house or anything drastic. He was merely suggesting that they make the most of the time they had left before she returned to Florida.

And, of course, he was right—she didn't have to divulge anything to his family that she didn't want to. That was her conscience getting in the way, holding her back—same way it had all these months.

When the pad of Wynn's thumb brushed her palm, her fingers twitched.

"If you won't see me again," he said, "could I ask you to do just one thing?"

"What's that?"

"Leave me with a kiss."

Her breath caught. He was looking at her so intently.

"Just one?" she asked.

He brought her close. "You decide."

The moment his mouth covered hers, longing flooded her every cell. The night before, she had lain awake, too, imagining he was there beside her, stroking and toying and pleasing her the way only Wynn seemed to know how. She'd reinvented the moment before she'd said good-night, but rather than closing the door, she'd grabbed his tie and dragged him inside.

Now, with his mouth working a slow-burn rhythm over hers and that hot pulse at her core beginning to throb, she felt boneless—beaten. *One kiss*. She didn't want to stop at just one. But she hadn't lost her mind completely. This wasn't the place or the time.

Breathless, she broke away. "Wynn, I need to go."

"I want you to stay." His lips grazed hers. "*You* want to stay."

"Anyone could come in."

He strode across the room, locked the door, strode back. No more words. He only brought her close, and as his mouth captured hers and his embrace tightened, suddenly time and place didn't matter.

He shifted his big hands and gripped her on either side of her waist. He slowly lifted her and as her feet left the floor, he made certain that he pressed her against him extra close. Then their mouths slipped apart and rather than looking up at him, now she was looking down.

When he sat her on the desk, his mouth found hers again—a scorching all-bets-are-off caress. His palms drove all the way down her back, and as his hands wedged under her behind, she blindly unbuttoned part of his shirt. Slipping a hand into the opening, she sighed at the feel of crisp hair matted over hard, steamy flesh.

One hand slipped out from beneath her, slicing down the back of her thigh until he gripped the back of that knee. As the kiss deepened, she wrenched at the knot of his tie. When collar buttons proved too stubborn, she tugged harder and they popped off. She unraveled the shirt from his shoulders at the same time he pushed against her, tilting her back, bringing her knee back, too.

When she lay flat on the desk, his mouth broke from hers. He shifted enough to peel the shirt off his back. As he moved forward, he pushed up her skirt. He positioned himself between her thighs and his mouth met hers again.

Arching up, she clutched at his chest while a big warm hand drove between them and found the front of her briefs. When she bucked, wanting more, the kiss intensified before two thick fingers slid lower between thin silk and warm skin. As he explored her slick folds, the pad of his thumb grazed the bead at the top of her cleft. She bit her lip to contain a sigh. *All those sizzling nerve endings.* Then he pressed that spot with just the right pressure and a burning arrow shot straight to her core.

She was clinging to his shoulders when he slipped his hand out from her briefs. She pushed up against him until she was sitting upright, her hands colliding with his in their race to unbutton her blouse. As he wrangled the sleeves off her shoulders, she scooted back more on the desk.

But then their eyes connected, and a hushed surreal moment passed. He drew down a breath and seemed to gather himself before he urged her back down. Finding her right leg, he raised it at an angle almost perpendicular to the desk. Taking his time, he slid off her high heel before his palms sailed down either side of her calf, her thigh. Then he slipped off the other heel and raised that leg, too. He dropped a lingering kiss on one instep and then repeated the caress on the other.

Holding her ankles on either side of his ears, he let his gaze travel all the way down her body. He studied her rumpled skirt and, higher, the swell of her breasts encased in two scraps of lace. Releasing her legs, he scooped one breast out from its cup. Between finger and thumb, he twirled the nipple, lightly plucked the tip. When the tingling, beautiful burn was almost too much to bear, she reached out, inviting him down.

His tongue circled her nipple, flicked around the edges, before teasing the tip. As his mouth covered the peak and he lightly sucked, she sighed and knotted her fingers in his hair. She murmured about how amazing he was—how incredible he made her feel—as the pulse in her womb beat stronger and the fuse linking pleasure to climax grew alarmingly short. She adored the suction, the careful graze of his teeth but, so much more now, she needed him to open her—to enter and to fill her.

He shifted his attention to scooping her other breast from the bra. As he turned his head and his mouth worked its magic there, his hands slid under her shoulders. When he drew her toward him, she was raised up and then off the desk to stand before him. His mouth left her nipple with a soft smacking sound before he unsnapped her bra and released her skirt's clasp. The skirt dropped at the same time she shrugged off her bra and he whipped open his belt, unzipped his pants and fell back into his big leather chair.

She was down to hold-up stockings and briefs. He tipped forward and two fingers slid under the elastic strips resting on each hip. He pressed a moist kiss high on her leg just shy of her sex before he dragged the silk triangle all the way down. The tip of his tongue drew a slow, moist path across her bikini line as a palm filed up over her belly, her abdomen and then high enough to weigh one breast. When his tongue trailed lower, fire shot through her body. Gripping the hand kneading her breast, she dropped her head to press kisses on each fingertip.

Reclining, he drew her along with him until she straddled his lap. She hadn't noticed until now but he'd already found a foil-wrapped condom. To give him room, she grabbed the back of the chair and pushed up on her knees—which relocated her sex at the level of his mouth.

As he rolled protection on, he dotted kisses on one side of her mound then the other. Then he guided her down until the tip of his length nudged at her opening and eased a little inside.

The rush was so direct, so entirely perfect, Grace shuddered from her crown to the tips of her still-stockinged feet. He held her in that position, hovering, as his lips trailed her throat and he told her how much he'd missed her, missed this. When she clasped his ears and planted her lips over his, he eased her down a little more.

He rotated her hips in a way that put pressure on an internal hot spot that already felt ready to combust. When he eased out and in again, deeper this time, a trail of effervescent sensations drifted through the expressways of her veins. Hands on her hips, he urged her up until the tip of his erection was cupped by her folds. Then he brought her down again, more firmly, filling her completely this time.

The slam hit her everywhere and all at once. Her walls squeezed at the same time her head dropped into his hair. She wanted to keep him there, buried deep inside of her. She needed to hold onto the fringes of this feeling that let her know she was already hanging so close to that edge. With each and every breath, the world dropped farther away. She'd become only the rhythm beating in her brain, ordering her movements, stoking those flames.

As his tempo increased, her breath came in snatches. When a thrust hit that hot spot again, she let go of the chair and pulled his face up to hers. Her fingers knotted in his hair as their tongues darted in and out.

And then his movements slowed to an intense, controlled grind. When his tongue probed deeper, everything started to close in.

As Wynn thrust forward, she flopped back, wrapping her legs around his hips. When he moved harder, faster, she couldn't hold on. The force of her orgasm threw her back more.

As she stiffened, he drew her toward him, his arms holding her like a vice. When his mouth closed over hers, it only pushed her higher. She came apart, every fiber, every thought. She felt as if she'd been released into the tightest, brightest place that had ever existed. Nothing could interrupt the energy, nothing could defuse the thrill. Nothing… except…

Except maybe…

She frowned.

That sound.

Who was knocking on the door?

With the throbs petering out, reality seeped back in. She was crouched over Wynn, naked but for stockings, one of which was pushed down below the knee. Wynn at least still had his pants on, even if they weren't covering what they normally would.

When the knock came again and a man called out, she looked to Wynn, who put a finger to her lips. A sound filtered back from the other side of the room—the knob rattling. With her eyes, she asked, *What do we do?* and he gave her a *don't worry* look. Then the rattling stopped.

After a long moment, he whispered, "Let's pretend that didn't happen—the interruption, I mean." He stole a deep kiss. "Not this."

When he leaned in close and flashed her his slanted smile again, she turned her head, let out a breath and gathered herself. The lights were so bright. Had the person at the door heard any telltale sighs or groans?

She held her damp brow. "We got carried away."

He was nibbling her shoulder. "Uh-huh." His mouth slid up her throat. "Let's do it again."

Pulling back, she gaped at him and almost laughed. "You're crazy."

"It's my office. My company." He dropped a kiss on her chin, on her jaw. "I can be crazy if I want."

He pulled her closer and she felt him still thick and rigid inside of her. She'd been so involved in her own responses, she hadn't thought about him, although now she got the impression he was dangerously close to climaxing, too. But what if that knocking came again? Wondering if someone was still hovering around out there wasn't so great for the mood.

As if reading her thoughts, he nodded toward a connecting door. "I have a suite through there I use if I've had a long day and feel too beat to drag myself home."

"Let me guess." She arched a brow. "There's a bed."

His lips grazed hers. "Coming right up."

Later, as she and Wynn lay in the adjoining suite's bed, her blood hummed with warmth, as if every drop were coated in soft golden light. She felt so high, she couldn't imagine enduring a less satisfied state. She wouldn't worry about whether this had been a dumb move or merely inevitable. Now that Wynn had finished to supreme satisfaction what had begun in his office, Grace only wanted to bask in the afterglow…although she did feel unsettled about one thing.

With his arm draped around her shoulders, Wynn was nuzzling her crown while Grace snuggled in and asked, "Any idea who knocked on the door?"

"Christopher Riggs. I put him on here at my father's recommendation. Guess he had something he wanted to share."

"Something urgent?"

"Right now, this takes priority."

When he leaned forward and grinned, she pushed up on an elbow. "It sounded urgent."

He lay back and cradled his head. "He's full of ideas. Good ones. But nothing that can't wait till tomorrow."

When Wynn rolled over and his mouth once again covered hers, thoughts of Christopher Riggs evaporated. All that mattered were the shimmering emotions wrapping around her body and her mind. She could lie here with Wynn like this all night, but she winced at the thought of slinking out of the building after dawn. He might not like it, either.

When his mouth gradually left hers, his strong arms bundled her closer still. "I'll book another ticket for Sydney."

Cupping his raspy jaw, she brushed her lips back and forth over his. "I haven't said yes yet."

"But you will," he said with a confidence that made her feel somehow safe.

Before they'd begun to make love outside in his office, yes, she had decided to change her mind and go with him. Naturally his family would be curious about her life, but she didn't need to answer any questions she felt uncomfortable with.

Wynn's hand trailed down over her hip. "And we could spend more time together," he murmured against her lips. "More time like this."

Mmm. So nice. "You've convinced me," she said, brushing her smile over his. "I'll go."

His dark eyes lit and his smile grew. "I'll let Cole know tomorrow. Teagan will be stoked, and you'll love Tate. I think he's the one I'm looking forward to seeing again most. Dad must be counting down the days."

Did Wynn mean *counting down the days to the wedding*, or, "Has Tate been away?"

He hesitated, frowned and then propped himself up. "There's been some trouble back home."

He relayed details surrounding the problems Guthrie Hunter had experienced with a stalker. Unbelievable, Hollywood thriller type stuff.

"Tate was with Dad the day he was assaulted," Wynn

said. "We all thought it best that he be removed from that situation until they catch the guy. He stayed with Teagan first. Now he's with Dex."

"But he's going back to Australia next week, right? So, the stalker's been caught?"

"Not yet."

The pieces of the puzzle began to slot into place. She thought back. "Last night, when I assumed your brother's wedding would be a huge event…"

"It was decided that a small and therefore more easily controlled ceremony would be wise."

"So where's the wedding being held?"

"At the family home. They have a huge mansion over-looking the harbor. Obviously security will be of the highest priority. We have a top gun in the security world on the job. Brandon Powell is the best."

"Does my dad know about all this?" She hadn't seen any reports in the news. Obviously the Hunters had worked to keep the whole ordeal as quiet as possible.

"We've tried to keep it out of the media, but our fathers have spoken about it. Brock and I touched on the subject the other night, too."

Clearly the problem was serious—serious enough for a father to ship his youngest halfway around the world. What lay behind it all?

Wynn eased out a breath. "It's been months since that last incident, and the investigation is still going strong. If anyone thought there was any possibility of danger, Tate wouldn't be coming home."

"So, he's staying home for good?"

Wynn hesitated. "Not decided yet." His hand wrapped around hers. "I'm looking forward to seeing all the family again together. It'll be good having you be a part of that, too."

An odd feeling crept into her stomach. The idea of some

psycho searching out Guthrie Hunter, intent on doing major harm… It chilled her to the bone. On the other hand, Wynn seemed so certain that everything was under control. Hopefully Brandon Powell would find some answers, and fast.

Six

Brock Munroe commuted to Manhattan from Long Island each weekday for work. However, rather than ask her father for a lift, Grace hired a car to drive herself to the French-inspired manor she'd once called home.

On returning to New York last week, Grace had, of course, arranged to drop by. That day she'd been welcomed by fifty of the family's closest friends. Everyone had been so careful not to mention Sam. Even her mother, perhaps his biggest fan, seemed to try. But Grace wouldn't run the risk of being swamped again. She'd decided that on subsequent visits, including this one, she'd show up unannounced.

Grace drove up the wide, graveled drive and took in the manicured lawns and the manor's grand provincial theme. A moment later, the Munroe's soaring front door was opened by a woman who had just joined the house staff earlier that year.

"Miss Munroe!" With a wide smile, the housekeeper

ushered her through. "Your mother will be pleased to see you."

"Thanks, Jenn." Grace stepped onto the white-oak hardwood flooring of the double-story foyer. Absorbing the familiar smells of cypress beams and jasmine-scented incense, she glanced around. "Where is she?"

"The sunroom. I need to consult on the dinner menu with your mother. I'll walk you through." Jenn headed down the hall. "Your sister's here."

"Tilly?"

The youngest Munroe girl was in her final year of high school. Popular as well as a brain, Tilly seemed to breeze through life, blithely knocking down whatever obstacle got in her way.

"Matilda's upstairs," Jenn said, "dancing to one of her routines, I expect." Pointing her rubber-soled toes, the housekeeper gave Grace a cheeky grin. "I learned dance when I was young." She looked ahead again. "Rochelle's here, too."

Grace's step faltered and she groaned. Guess she'd catch up with everyone, then.

A pattering of footfalls filtered down the hall before a little girl turned a corner and trundled into view, her mahogany curls bouncing in a cloud around her head. When Grace's five-year-old niece saw her, April squealed. Putting her head down, she ran in earnest, sending layers of play necklaces jangling and clinking around her neck. Laughing, Grace knelt and caught her niece as she ploughed into her open arms. April smacked a kiss on her cheek.

"The bell rang and Granma sent me." April held her aunt's face in tiny, dimpled hands. "We didn't know it'd be *you!*"

They rubbed noses. Then Grace pushed up to her full height and took her niece's hand.

"What've you been up to, princess?" Grace asked as they strolled on.

"Daddy's working hard. He has lots of people to fix."

"Your daddy's a surgeon. Very important job."

"Uh-huh. He's busy." Innocent brown eyes turned up to meet her aunt's. "Mommy says he has to stay away a while."

At the hospital? Or was Trey at a medical convention? No doubt, she'd hear the entire story from Rochelle soon—one more treat in her sister's chocolate box of "perfect married life" tales.

Nearing the sunroom, April skipped on ahead. "Gracie's here!" she called.

Looking exquisite in an apricot jersey dress, Suzanne Munroe pushed up from a white brocade sofa. Grace couldn't remember a time when her mother had looked anything other than exquisite. As a girl, Grace wanted to grow up to be just like her and had sought out her mother's approval in everything. If Mom suggested she tie ribbons in her hair, ribbons it would be. If her mother proposed singing lessons, Grace would do her best to reach those high notes. As she'd gotten older, she'd come to understand that she had her own identity and dreams to pursue.

The dynamics of their relationship had needed to change.

But apron strings made of steel weren't easy to break. As her mother crossed over, Grace imagined those same high-tensile tendrils reaching out to coil around her now. But at age twenty-six, whose fault was that—her mother's for not listening, or her own for not making herself heard?

Grace walked into an extra-long hug from her mother at the same time Suzanne Munroe instructed Jenn to come back with some suggestions for tonight's menu, which, she reminded the housekeeper, needed to be free of all nut and egg products. April was allergic. Then, pulling back, her mother gestured toward the stash of costume and kids' jewelry littering a coffee table. Lit by afternoon sunshine steaming in through a bank of picture windows, piles of red, green and yellow "diamonds" glittered like a children's book treasure.

Her mother explained. "April and I have been trying on our jewels."

Grace crouched beside April, who was holding up another bundle of necklaces in front of her pink pinafore bodice.

"When I was young, I loved dressing up," Grace told her niece.

"You had more costumes than regular clothes," her mom pointed out. "One minute you were a princess, then a mermaid...the next, a bride..."

On the surface, that last remark was harmless; however, Grace didn't miss the lamenting tone. The connection. Sam hadn't been the high-flying lawyer or doctor her upper-crust mother might have preferred for a son-in-law, but his family was extremely wealthy and, having saved two young boys from a raging inferno a couple of years ago, he'd been known as a hero. Before Sam's accident, how many times had her mother announced that she couldn't wait to see Grace in a white gown and veil? Couldn't wait for her to make them all happy as a bride?

"Your costumes...can I have the princess one?" April cupped the top of her head. "Does it have a crown?"

"That was a long time ago," Grace replied. It went way back to a time when she'd first known Wynn Hunter.

Her mother took Grace's hands. "I brought Nan back with me from Maine. She's been asking about you."

Grace remembered how frail her grandmother had looked three months ago, one hand resting on her husband's rose-strewn coffin, the other pressing a lace handkerchief to her cheek.

"How is she?" Grace asked.

"Still feeling lost." Her mother gave Grace a "you'd understand" look before flicking a glance toward the stairs. "She's napping."

"Nanna naps all the time," April lamented, slotting a multicarat "ruby" on her middle finger and then scooting off up the stairs, presumably to check.

"When she sees you," her mother went on, "I'm sure she'll perk up. You'll stay for dinner." She dropped her chin. "Now, I won't take no for an answer."

Grace was about to say that of course she'd stay—she also wanted to ask where Rochelle was hiding—but then two items resting on the mantle of the French limestone fireplace drew her attention and the words dried on her tongue. When her mother's attention shifted to the mantle, too, her shoulders slumped. Crossing to the fireplace, her mother studied the photos—one of Grandpa, the other of Sam.

"Last week, before you called in," her mother said, returning with Sam's photo in hand, "I put this away. Your father didn't think you needed reminding. Of course, I put it back out after you left." She smiled down at the picture and sighed. "He always looked so handsome in his uniform."

When she held the frame out to her, Grace automatically stepped away. Yes, Sam was kind and brave and handsome. He was a natural with kids, including April. But her father was right. She didn't need reminding. She lived with enough memories.

But she couldn't go back—change what had already played out. She could only move forward, and now seemed the time to let her mother know precisely that, and as plainly as she could.

"I'm going to Australia," Grace announced. "Leaving next week."

Her mother's brow pinched. "Why? With whom?"

"With Wynn Hunter."

While Grace's heart hammered against her ribs, her

mother blinked several times before a smile appeared, small and wry.

"Your father mentioned that he'd run into Wynn. But now, you're…what? Seeing each other?"

"His brother Cole's getting married in Sydney. Wynn asked if I'd like to go. It'll be nice to catch up with Teagan."

"I saw Wynn at his mother's funeral a few years back. At his father's subsequent wedding, too. He seemed to have grown into a fine young man." Her focus dipped to the photo again, and then she arched a brow. "Is it serious?"

Grace could truthfully admit, "Not serious at all."

"So, you're not having a…well," her voice dropped, "a relationship?"

Grace thought about it. "That would depend on your definition."

"I see. More a fling." Her mother's look was dry—*wounded*—as she crossed to slot the frame back on the mantle. "It's none of my business…." Then she took a breath and swung back around. "But, I'm sorry, Grace. I can't say I approve. Those types of affairs might seem like a harmless distraction. Except someone always gets hurt."

A movement near the stairs drew Grace's eye. Rochelle was wandering over. Her face was almost as pale as the white linen shirt she wore. With a fluid gait, her mother joined her.

"My God, Rochelle," Grace murmured, "what's wrong?"

When their mother asked, "Is April with Nan?" Rochelle found energy enough to nod and settle on the sofa. Sitting, too, Grace held her older sister's arm and examined her blotched complexion.

"Shell, you've been crying."

Rochelle shuddered out a defeated breath. "Trey's had an affair. He's gone."

The room seemed to tilt. Grace remembered April's comment about her daddy needing to stay away. So, he'd left the family home? Or had Rochelle kicked him out? But none of it made sense. Those two had the perfect marriage, the kind of union their parents held up as a shining example. The kind of relationship their mother wanted for all her girls. The kind of bond Grace had once tried to convince herself she'd had with Sam.

In the past, Rochelle's stories revolving around her sparkling life had grated. Still, Grace loved her sister. She adored her niece. Now, as tears filled Rochelle's desolate green eyes, Grace wanted to help if she could.

"Do you know the other woman?"

"A nurse. A friend." Rochelle set her vacant stare on the far wall. "I had no idea. She held April's hand while we all watched fireworks on Independence Day."

When a tear slid down Rochelle's cheek, Grace folded her sister in her arms; she couldn't imagine how dazed and sick to her stomach she must feel. And if Trey had confessed… Was the affair still on?

"Is Trey still seeing this woman?"

"Doesn't matter whether he is or not." Their mother's elegant fingers clutched her throat as she sniffed. "The damage is done."

Grace considered her mother's indignant look and made the leap: *this* was an example of a fling's dire consequences.

Another, younger voice boomed out across the room. "Yay! Gracie's here!"

With a hip-hop gait, Tilly entered the room. Given those shocks of black and burgundy hair, she might have stuck her finger in a power socket. Grace noted that Rochelle was swiping at her cheeks, putting on a brave face—the stoic Munroe way.

So, Tilly didn't know?

Tilly was blinking from one to the other. "What's up?"

Her mother busied herself tidying the jewels. "Everything's fine."

Tilly crossed her arms. "Doesn't look fine."

"Grace is staying for dinner." Taking control of the situation, as usual, their mother moved to slip an arm around her youngest daughter's waist. "Jenn can prepare a big roast with sweet potato rounds for appetizers. Oh, and how about a strawberry torte to finish?"

While Rochelle looked flattened, Tilly seemed confused and Grace couldn't help but recall: torte had been Sam's favorite.

When Brock Munroe arrived home that evening, Suzanne took him aside, presumably to relay the news regarding Trey's infidelity. During dinner, their father remained stony-faced, poor Nan and Rochelle barely spoke and Tilly quietly observed the whole scene. Their mother overcompensated with a slew of chatter—except when it came to the subject of Grace's visit to Sydney.

While her father patted her hand and said the trip sounded nice—he obviously didn't see a problem with regard to Guthrie Hunter's recent difficulties or her accompanying Wynn over there—the tension at the other end of the long table built.

After plates were cleared, Nan excused herself, April was put to bed and Grace decided some fresh air and alone time were in order.

She'd bought a notebook the day before. Now with that book and a rug tucked under one arm, she ventured out onto the back partly enclosed terrace, which overlooked the pool. She rested an elbow on the wicker chair's arm, tapped the pen against her chin and let her mind wind back. In these surroundings with her family—here and now seemed the best place to start.

Grace was a world away, adding to how events had unraveled the night of Sam's accident, when she was interrupted.

"What are you writing?"

Snapping back to the present, Grace focused on Rochelle, who had appeared beside a row of potted sculptured shrubs. She half fibbed. "Working on an exercise."

"For speech therapy?"

"It's definitely about getting a message clear."

Once she'd begun to jot down her thoughts, she'd experienced a kind of catharsis. Now she wondered why she hadn't thought to do this before.

"How're you feeling?" Grace asked, closing the notebook.

"Less shaken than I was earlier," Rochelle admitted. "April's eyes were itching before she nodded off."

"Allergies?"

"Maybe just tired. She's had a big day." She gestured toward a chair. "Can I join you?"

"I'd like that."

"I came from Tilly's room." Rochelle lowered into a chair. "She wanted to know what was wrong."

"You told her?"

"She might be seventeen but she's not a child. She said she'd come stay over the holidays if April and I needed company."

"Tilly's always been a good kid."

"And the only one in this family who Mom can't corral. That girl has the stubbornness of a mule."

"Of *ten* mules."

They both grinned before a distant look clouded Rochelle's eyes. Bowing her head, she studied her left hand. The enormous diamond on her third finger caught the artificial light, casting shifting prisms over her face.

"It's hard to believe it was all an illusion," Rochelle murmured. "That he doesn't really love me."

"Did Trey say that?"

"A person doesn't eat off another plate if he's happy

with the dish he has at home. This year, I wanted to try for another baby. Trey said to wait." Biting her lip, she let her head rock back. "I'm such an idiot."

"None of this is your fault. No one deserves that kind of betrayal."

"Mom didn't want Trey and I to get married. She thought he was a flirt. Women respond when he walks into a room." Rochelle's watery eyes blinked slowly as her mouth formed a bittersweet smile. "I felt lucky."

They sat in silence for a while, studying the shadows beyond the terrace, before Rochelle spoke again.

"I'm sorry I wasn't much of a help when Sam passed away. I liked him."

Yeah. "Everyone liked Sam."

"But you didn't love him, did you, Grace? Not deeply and with all your heart."

Grace froze as a surreal sensation swept through her body. She stared at her sister. "You knew?"

"He looked at you the same way I look at Trey—with adoration, and hope."

When Rochelle hugged herself, Grace threw one side of the rug over for her to share.

"If he hadn't died," Rochelle said, snuggling in, "do you think you'd have got married?"

"No." Grace shook her head. "Even if everyone else thought we should."

"I always wondered why Trey asked me."

"Maybe because you're smart and beautiful—"

"And filled with insecurities? You can't imagine how tiring it is, pretending everything's amazingly wonderful when you wonder if your husband thinks your hips are monstrous, or you're not witty enough, and it's a matter of time before someone finds out you're a big fat fraud."

Queen Rochelle had never thought she was good enough?

The stories about her fabulous life were all a front? Guess they weren't so different, after all.

"We all have insecurities," Grace admitted. "At some stage, we all pretend."

"All those late, long hours…" Rochelle's nostrils flared. "He's probably had other flings."

There was that word again. That jolt. But her situation with Wynn was a thousand times different from Rochelle's. No cheating was involved—although in some ways they were each still attached to other people: her to Sam's memory, and Wynn to his beautiful ex.

Wynn had said that woman was in his past and yet she'd seen the emotion in his eyes. His ex had broken it off. Had she cheated on him the way Trey had cheated on Rochelle? Sam would never have done such a thing. Wynn, either.

Surely not.

"When are you leaving for Australia?" Rochelle asked.

Grace was still shivering from that last thought. "Monday. Mom's not pleased about it."

"Daddy thinks it's a good idea. I do, too. It's been years but I liked Wynn Hunter, even if he seemed a little intense."

"He's still intense, but in a different, steady-simmer kind of way. There's something about him, Shell. Something… hypnotic." Grace's smile wavered. "Almost dangerous."

"Different from Sam, then?" Rochelle joked.

"In pretty much every way."

When Grace shifted, the notebook slipped. Rochelle caught it and handed it back. Thinking about the secret contained within those pages, Grace ran a fingertip over the cover. What would her family say if they knew the whole story? Given Wynn's past, what would *he* say?

"I'm still not one hundred percent sure about going to Sydney," she admitted. "Cole's getting married. Apparently Dex is besotted with his fiancée. Cupid's shooting arrows all over the place where the Hunters are concerned."

She thought of her friend Amy and her bubbling enthusiasm over Wynn's kiss the previous weekend.

"I know the kind of atmosphere weddings create," Grace said. "Everyone's in love with the idea of being in love, and I'm over fending off other people's expectations."

"I'm not the one to give advice here but, Gracie, don't worry about what anyone thinks. You're a different person from the girl who started dating Sam. Hell, I'm different from the person who fell head over heels seven years ago for Trey. Back then, I felt giddy—so happy. Now I feel as if I've fallen in some deep, dark pit."

Grace's heart squeezed for her sister. It had been hard losing Sam, but he wasn't the father of her child. Regardless of this bombshell, Rochelle had loved her husband. Still, Rochelle could find comfort in the knowledge that people cared about her, and would look after both her and April, no matter what.

Grace held her sister's gaze. "You'll be okay. You know that, right?"

"Yeah. I know." Finding a brave smile, Rochelle leaned her head on her little sister's shoulder. "We both will."

Seven

The following week, the Qantas airbus Grace and Wynn had boarded in New York landed safely at Sydney Airport. With luggage collected, the pair jumped into a luxury rental vehicle and headed for the Hunter mansion. Travelling over connecting roads with the convertible's soft top down, Grace sighed at the picture-perfect views.

Sydney's heart was its harbor, an enormous, mirror-blue expanse that linked town and suburbs via fleets of green-and-yellow ferries. Built on the capital's northeastern tip, the giant shells of the world-famous Sydney Opera House reflected the majesty of a city whose mix of skyscrapers and parkland said "smart and proud and new." The mint-fresh air and southern-hemisphere sunshine left Grace feeling clean and alive, even after a twenty-odd hour flight.

She'd been a little anxious over whether Wynn's wedding-focused family might cast rose petals in their path, or if that crazy stalker situation would prove to be less contained than Wynn hoped and believed; if some madman wanted to harm

Wynn's father, what better time to creep out from the shadows than when the entire family was together and off guard.

But with a warm breeze pulling through her hair and the promise of nothing but relaxation, mixed with some sight-seeing adventures, she was feeling good about her decision. Nevertheless, when the BMW swung into the Hunter mansion's massive circular drive, Grace found herself drawing down a deep breath.

A member of the house staff answered the door and they were shown to a lounge room that was filled with people. An older silver-haired man, whom Grace recognized as Guthrie Hunter, stepped forward and put his arms around Wynn in a brief but affectionate man-hug before stepping back to assess his son's face.

"You look well, Wynn."

"You, too."

Grace heard relief in Wynn's voice; given those escalating threats on his father's life, no doubt he expected the wear to show.

And then all eyes were on her. Grace tacked up her smile at the same time Wynn introduced her.

"Everyone, meet Grace Munroe." Grinning, he cocked a brow. "Or, should I say, meet her again?"

An attractive woman around Grace's age romped up to hug her, long and tight. With thick blond hair pulled back in a ponytail, she smelled of oatmeal shampoo. Her tanned arms were strong, her body superfit and lean in her hot pink exercise singlet. Grace let loose a laugh and pulled back.

"Teagan, you need to be on the cover of your own health and fitness magazine!"

"Blame the day job." Teagan mock flexed a biceps. "I can't wait to catch up on all your news." She slid a knowing glance Wynn's way. "That is, if my dear brother will let you out of his sight for a minute."

Grace waited for Wynn to somehow brush the remark

aside. Instead he looped an arm around her waist and gave everyone a lopsided smile—a kind of confirmation. Which felt nice, but also wrong. She hadn't wanted to give anyone that impression. They weren't dating. Or at least they didn't have any long-term agendas, and she didn't want to have to fend off any open speculation that they did.

But then Wynn gave her a squeeze and she read the message in his eyes. *Relax.* Guess she was looking up-tight. Overreacting.

A man stepped up, acknowledging her with an easy smile and tip of his head. He had hair dark and glossy like Wynn's, classically chiseled features and ocean-green eyes…

"You, I recognize," Grace exclaimed. "Cole, right?"

"The pigtails are gone," Cole joked, "but you haven't lost that cheeky grin." He beckoned someone over—a stunning woman with a waterfall of dark hair and eyes only for this man. She held out a hand—slender and manicured.

"I'm Taryn, Cole's blushing bride-to-be." Her Australian accent was pitch-perfect and welcoming. "We're so glad you could both make it."

"Wynn's excited about being here for the wedding, see-ing everyone," Grace admitted. "I am, too."

Another man sauntered up. This brother's hair was sun-streaked, and his expression was open for all who cared to see. Those tawny eyes—like a lion's—were unmistakable.

"I'm Dex," he said, "Let me introduce you to the love of my life."

Laughing, a statuesque redhead dressed in modest denim cut-offs stepped up and shook Grace's hand heart-ily. "Shelby Scott. Pleased to meet you."

Grace detected a hint of a twang. "Texas?"

"I was born in a real nice place in Oklahoma," Shelby said with pride.

"Mountain Ridge," Dex added. "Ranch country. You

should see her in a pair of spurs." With his strong arms linked around her, Shelby angled to give him a censoring look. Dex only snatched a kiss that lingered until a boy with Dex's same tawny-colored eyes and wearing a bright red T-shirt, broke through the wall of adults.

"Are you going to marry Wynn?" The boy's shoulders bobbed up and down. "All my brothers are getting hitched."

Dex ruffled the boy's hair. "Hey, buddy, rein it in a little. We don't want to scare Grace off just yet."

It seemed like a room full of curious eyes slid back toward Grace as the boy considered, and then asked again. "Well, are you?"

Wynn hunkered down. "Tate, when Grace and I first met, she was around your age. Crazy, huh?"

Shoving his hands into the back pockets of his shorts, Tate eyed Grace as if he truly did think it was mad, but also interesting. "I like dinosaurs," he told her. "Do you?"

Kneeling down, Grace tried to think. "I don't know any."

"That's okay." When Tate smiled, Grace saw he'd lost a tooth. "I have lots. I'll show you."

Taking her hand, Tate yanked but his father stopped him short. "Son, our latest guest hasn't met all the family yet."

Another woman—a *very* pregnant woman—entered the room. Her high cheekbones and large, thickly-lashed eyes bespoke classic beauty—or would have if not for the grimace, which seemed to have something to do with the way she held the small of her back. This must be Eloise, Grace thought. Wynn's stepmother, although she looked young enough to be a sister.

"I swear, if I don't have this child soon," Eloise said, "I'll collapse. I can't carry this twenty-pound bowling ball around inside of me much longer."

As Eloise ambled nearer, Cole's shoulders inched up. Taryn slipped an arm through her fiancé's, as if reminding him she was there, a support. Grace wondered.

What's that all about?

Stopping before the newly arrived couple, Eloise dredged up a put-upon smile and Wynn stepped forward to brush a kiss on his stepmom's cheek. As he drew away, Eloise looked to Grace as if she expected the same greeting from her. Grace only nodded hello before saying, "Thanks for having me in your home," and then, "Can I ask—do you know what you're having?"

"I've prayed for a daughter. Every woman wants one." Eloise's gaze flicked to Teagan, who was squatting, tying Tate's shoelace. "*Another* daughter, I mean." She set her weight on her other leg. "After that long trip, you both must need a good lie down. Your old room's all ready for you, honey," she said to Wynn.

"Barbecue's happening around five," Cole added.

"I'll bring a dinosaur," Tate said.

A moment later, Wynn was ushering Grace up a grand staircase, then down a corridor that led to a separate wing of the house. His "room" looked more like a penthouse suite. Standing in the center of the enormous space, which included a king-size bed, Grace set her hands on her hips.

"You had all this to yourself growing up?" she asked.

"Doesn't mean I sat around, bathing in milk and ringing the butler's bell."

"No?" She turned to face him.

"I worked very hard at my studies and sport."

She wandered over. "Wanna show me your trophies?"

"I wanna show you something."

His arms circled her and his mouth covered hers. It was a stirring kiss. Warm and good and…somehow different. Must be because of the surroundings. As his lips left hers, she let her eyes drift open and memories of the Hunters and that Colorado Christmas came flooding back. One memory in particular. She pressed her lips together to cover a laugh.

"I can still see you gnashing your teeth over that snowman's hat not sitting straight."

He pretended to scowl. "Because you and Teagan kept messing with it when my back was turned."

She didn't cover her laugh this time. "You were so darn easy to stir."

When she bopped his nose, he jerked to take a bite at that finger. "You were lucky I remained a gentleman."

"I don't remember you behaving in a gentlemanly fashion. You'd go all stiff and mutter that I needed a good spanking."

His lips came close to graze up the slope of her throat. "I'm feeling and thinking the same thing now."

While his tongue tickled her earlobe, the zipper on the back of her dress whirred down. She felt the cool air, and then a warm palm slid in over her skin before skating down toward her rear. Closing her eyes, Grace let her head rock back.

"I thought we were going to rest before dinner," she said, "not play."

"Either way, we need to get out of these clothes."

He slid the dress off one shoulder, she handled the other shoulder, and the dress fell to the floor.

Since that evening in his office, they'd seen each other regularly. Whenever they got together, inevitably they would end up in bed, exploring each other's bodies, discovering what the other liked best, and then finding new ways to top that. Like that thing his mouth was doing now to the lower sweep of her neck. The gentle tug of his teeth on her skin felt light and yet deep enough to ignite a set of nerve endings directly connected to her core.

But today they'd been travelling around the clock. Her body was pleading for a warm shower and some rest.

She stepped out of the dress pooled around her ankles and headed for the dresser, stopping twice to slip off each shoe while unfastening her heavy necklace. Laying the necklace on top of the dresser, she caught Wynn's reflection in the mirror. His gaze was dark and fixed upon her hips, the back of her briefs. He didn't look tired at all.

When he slipped off his shoes and moved up behind her, Grace's insides began to squeeze. His palms sailed over her bare shoulders, down her arms. Leaning back against his muscled heat, she breathed in his musky scent as two sets of fingers drew lines across her ribs before arrowing down, running light grooves over her belly to her briefs. He plucked at the elastic and murmured, "These need to come off."

As his fingers dived lower to comb and lightly tug at her curls, liquid heat filled her.

For comfort's sake, she hadn't worn a bra on the flight. In the mirror, through half-lidded eyes she watched him scoop up a breast with one hand while, lower, his other worked beneath her briefs. When he lightly pinched and rolled her nipple, she shivered, sighed and let her head drop to one side. The palm covering her mound urged her closer, pushing her bottom back to mold against him.

Then, knees bending, he began to slide down. She savored the feel of his defined abdomen, his chest and then chin, riding lower down her spine. When she felt his breath warm the small of her back, a finger hooked into the rear of her briefs and the silk was eased down to her knees. He dropped a lazy kiss on a hip then the slope of her bare behind. At the same time, the stroking between her legs delved deeper, slipping a little inside of her. She couldn't see his reflection in the mirror anymore—she only felt his mouth as it explored one side of her tush before trailing across the small of her back to sample the other side.

When his lips traveled lower and he kissed the sensitive area under the curve of one cheek, she held on to the dresser for support. Between her thighs, his fingertip rode up until he grazed and circled that sensitive nub. When he applied perfect pressure to the spot, stars shot off in her head before falling in a tingling, fire-tipped rain. She brought up one knee. Her briefs dropped from that leg before falling to rest around the other ankle. Pushing to his feet, he turned her around.

As his teeth danced down the column of her throat and his hands cupped her rear—lifting her at the same time they scooped her in—she gripped his shoulders. Steamy heat came through the fabric of his shirt to warm her palms. She brushed her wicked grin through his hair.

"Am I the only one getting undressed here?"

He paused. "Well, now, that could work."

He backed up a few steps while his gaze drank her in. Feeling desirable—and a little vulnerable—she leaned back against the dresser as his chest expanded on a deeply satisfied breath.

"You're perfect," he said. "I could stand here and just look at you all day."

Her cheeks were burning, not because she was embarrassed but because his words, the honesty in his voice, touched her in a way that left her wanting to please and tease him this much all the time.

With his focus glued on her, he backed up until his legs met the bed. After he threw back the covers and sat on the edge of the mattress, he beckoned her with a single curl of a finger. He wanted her to walk over and, given the glimmer in his eyes, he wanted her to take her time.

She took a breath and set one foot in front of the other; the closer she got, the more his dark eyes gleamed. When she was close enough, he reached to cup her neck and draw her down.

Her hair fell forward as her lips touched his. The contact was teasing—deliberately light. Her tongue rimmed the upper and lower seam of his mouth before she nipped his bottom lip and gently sucked. That's when his mouth took hers. As a strong arm coiled around her back, drawing her toward him more, she let her lips slide down and away from his at the same time she lowered to kneel at his feet.

She was positioned between his opened thighs, her mouth inches away from his chest. Taking her time, she released a shirt button, two and then three. Each time, she twirled her tongue over the newly exposed skin.

She pulled the shirttails out from his jeans, and when his shirt lay wide open and the bronzed planes of his chest and stomach were completely revealed, she started on his pants. With him leaning back, his arms supporting his weight, she flicked the snap, unzipped his fly. As she tugged at his jeans, her head dropped down.

Her tongue drew a lazy circle around his navel before she dotted moist kisses along the trail of hair that led to his boxer briefs. When she grazed her teeth over the bulge waiting there, his chest gave an appreciative rumble and he leaned back more, propping his weight on his elbows. Her fingers curled inside his briefs.

She dug out his engorged shaft and whirled a finger around the naked tip before her head lowered and her mouth covered him—barely an inch. Gripping his length at its base, her fist squeezed up as her mouth came down. Relishing the taste of him—the scent—she repeated the move again and again, taking her time, building the heat. He started to curl his pelvis up each time she came down while she squeezed him harder, took him deeper.

Too soon, he was sweeping her up and over, so that she lay flat on the bed. He whipped the shirt off his back and then retrieved a condom from his wallet, all before she could say she wasn't finished with him yet. When he tore open the foil, she took the condom and rolled the rubber all the way on. After ditching the jeans, he came back to kiss her, first thoroughly and then in one hungry, savoring snatch after another.

They were tangled up around each other, breathing ragged and energy pumped, when he urged her onto her side and pressed in against her—his front to her back. As he nuzzled the side of her neck, he drew her leg back over his and entered her in a "no prisoners" kind of way.

When he slid her leg back more, she stretched and ground against him. His thigh felt like a steel pylon. His chest was a slab of thermal rock. She grazed her cheek against his biceps as he held her and moved, setting up a rhythm that fed the pulse thumping in her throat and in her womb.

With his palm pressed against her belly, his fingers toyed with her curls. With each sweep, he grazed that uber-sensitive nub. The contact was maddening—drugging and delicious. When she was balanced on a precipice, oh-so ready to let go, he used his weight to tip her over.

Her leg uncoiled from around his thigh and her knee dug into the mattress at the same time her cheek pressed against the pillow. Settling in behind her, he began moving again, his pace faster now—fast enough for the front of his thighs to slap the backs of hers. This different angle changed the way that he filled her, placing a different pressure on a sensitive spot inside. The pleasure was so fragile and yet fierce—too exquisite to get her whirling mind around.

As his thrusts went deeper, he slid a palm under her belly to lift and press her closer. A searing heat compressed her core. A few more thrusts and she cried out as her fingers curled into the sheet and contractions swept in.

A heartbeat later, he gripped her hips and his strangled growl of release filled her ears.

Eight

"We don't have to go down," Wynn murmured as he bundled her close. "Go back to sleep."

After making love in his former bedroom, he and Grace had crashed. When his watch alarm had beeped a moment ago, he'd been stirred from a vivid dream—and Wynn rarely dreamed.

They were kids again, back in Colorado that Christmas long ago. There was a snowman with a screwy felt hat, and Wynn's scar was a fresh wound on his brow. Rather than blame an annoying brat for the gash, Wynn wondered if he'd tripped over his lace. He'd gone on to invite Grace—a lively, pretty thing—back to his parents' home in Australia.

"My brain feels full of cottonwool," Grace murmured against his chest as she tangled her leg around his. Her toes tickled the back of his knee. "But everyone's expecting us."

Inhaling the remnants of floral perfume mixed with the more alluring scent of *woman,* he kissed her crown. "They'll understand."

She glanced up. A line formed between her brows as she pushed hair away from her face. "We're not spending all our time here, right?"

"You mean in bed?"

She grinned. "In Sydney, dummy."

"I do have a surprise or two planned."

"Then I want to spend as much time as I can with Teagan while we're here." Grace shifted to lean up against the headboard of the bed. Her hair was mussed and still flopped over one side of her brow. "Do you know if she's seeing anyone? Anyone special?"

"Dex said he thought that she might be. But the man who catches our Ms. Independence will need to be darn determined."

She concurred. "Doesn't work until a girl wants to be caught."

"Like this?"

Craning up, he exacted one very thorough kiss that he didn't want to end.

When his mouth finally left hers, her breathing was heavier. The sheet had slipped from under her arms. Sliding down, he took a warm nipple deep into his mouth. His tongue was teasing the tip and his hand was snaking down over her belly when she gathered herself and pushed at his shoulders.

"I need a shower."

He spoke around the nipple. "You really don't."

Grace eased off the mattress and he lost possession of that breast. Then she was on her feet, standing in front of him with fists on her hips, as if that could put him off. He would have hooked her around her waist and brought her back—only he had a better idea.

Pushing up on an elbow, he cradled his cheek in his palm and nudged his chin. "Bathroom's that way."

Her eyes narrowed as if she suspected he might suddenly pounce, but he only smiled.

Two minutes later, Grace had the shower running and Wynn was swinging open the glass door to join her. When she turned to face him—her hair wet and rivulets of foam trailing over her body—her expression was not surprised. As he stepped in, she threaded slippery arms up and around his neck. With her breasts sliding and brushing against his ribs, she grazed her lips up his throat to his chin.

"You are so predictable," she said.

Grinning, he reached for the soap. "Don't bet on it."

"It's about time!"

Standing alongside of Wynn in the Hunter mansion's manicured backyard, Grace tracked down the source of the remark.

Inside an extravagant pavilion, two house staff flipped and prodded food grilling on a barbecue. A third attendant, carrying a drinks tray, was headed for the resort-style bar. Music played—a current hit from the U.K.—while a half dozen people splashed around in an enormous pool. Australian time put the hour at six o'clock, but the sun's heat and angle said they had a couple more hours of daylight yet to enjoy.

Grace heard the male voice that had greeted them earlier call again from the pool. "We were getting ready to come up and drag you two out of bed," Dex said as he splashed water in their direction.

Grace's cheeks heated, but it was a harmless remark. No one knew what she and Wynn had gotten up to. Even if they had guessed, they were all adults, with one exception.

In the pool, Tate was balanced on Cole's shoulders. He had his legs wrapped around his big brother's neck and was kicking in excitement. With a grin, Grace wondered where the dinosaurs were.

"Wynn!" the little boy called out. "I got a beach ball. We're in teams. You're with me!"

"Us against those two clowns?" Wynn called back, making a face as he gestured toward Cole and Dex. "Hardly seems fair."

Wynn wore a pair of square-leg black trunks that, along with his impressive upper body and long, strong legs, made Grace want to pounce on him again. She wore a bikini the color of the pool water with a matching resort-style dress cover. Now, the arm around her waist brought her closer as he asked, "Are you game?"

To splash around in that enormous pool with four boys?

Taryn was already out of the water, wringing her long dark hair, and Shelby was wading up the last of the arced pool stairs, right behind her. Teagan must be around somewhere, too.

"I have a feeling a lot of splashing and dunking is about to go down." She pinched his scratchy chin. "I'll go hang with the girls."

She craned up to catch his light kiss before returning her attention to the women. Shelby was motioning her over.

As Wynn ran up to the pool edge and did a cannonball, creating one hell of a splash, Grace accepted a glass of juice from the help and joined Shelby and Taryn near an extravagant outdoor setting.

Grace eyed Taryn's tan and smiled. "Wynn mentioned you and Cole had been off sailing."

Taryn wrapped a towel around her hips and folded herself into a chair. "A leisurely sweep around some Pacific islands." She sighed. "Pure heaven."

"When are you going again?" Shelby asked, grabbing a plastic flute of orange juice off the table before reclining into a chair.

"If all goes according to plan, we'll be able to fit it in just after the wedding." Taryn sent an adoring look over to where her fiancé was spiking a ball at Wynn. "Cole wants to start a family straightaway. Me, too."

Shelby leaned across and wrapped an arm around her future sister-in-law. "That's fabulous, hon."

Grace didn't feel she knew Taryn well enough to hug her. She saluted with her glass of juice instead.

Taryn cocked a brow Shelby's way. "Am I imagining it, or is Dex coming across as clucky, too?"

"Since looking after Tate these past weeks, he can't stop talking about having kids. We're really gonna miss that little guy if Guthrie decides he can stay." She sent Grace an apologetic look. "Sorry. We're leaving you out, running off at the mouth here."

Grace waved the apology away. She'd anticipated talk focusing on happily-ever-afters and babies. "I'm really glad for you both."

"Cole says you all knew each other as kids," Taryn said.

Grace glanced toward the pool. The three older brothers were play-wrestling, strong bodies glistening, muscles rippling, while Tate sat on the pool's edge, laughing and clapping his hands.

Grace admitted, "We've all changed a lot since then. I didn't recognize Wynn."

Leaning forward, Shelby straightened her bikini-top tie. Dex's fiancée had a presence—tall with striking features; she might have been a catwalk model rather than the nanny Dex had employed when he'd needed a sitter for Tate.

"They sure are big boys now," Shelby said. "What was Wynn like twenty years ago?"

"Earnest. Intense. He certainly didn't like girls. At least he didn't like me."

"And you?" Taryn asked. "Did you think he was cute even back then?"

"I had a tiny crush," Grace admitted. "A couple of times

I pinched his arm and ran away. The way he remembers it though, I harbored evil plans to ruin his life."

Taryn laughed. "True love," she said, while Shelby exclaimed, "It was meant to be, just like Dex and me. When we met, I was so off men. We took a long route round, but now I can't imagine life without him."

"I thought Cole was an arrogant jerk. He was so, my way or the highway." When Taryn came back from a memory that made her cheeks glow, she asked Grace, "How did you and Wynn meet up again?"

Grace cleared her throat and reinvented the truth.

"At a wedding," she said. "We talked, danced. He was leaving when the bride threw the bouquet. The flowers landed at my feet then skated across the floor right up to him. He brought them back and kissed me right in front of the crowd."

The words were out before Grace could think twice; she hadn't meant to reveal so much. Now Shelby was swooning while Taryn swirled her drink.

"A sentimental streak runs deep in the Hunter boys," Taryn said, "no matter how much they try to hide it at first. No question, they're all into family."

Grace focused on Wynn again. His arms out, he was encouraging Tate to dive back into the pool. *Yes*, she thought. If he ever got over the ex, Wynn would do well with a family of his own at some stage, and perhaps Taryn and Shelby were wondering if it might be with her. Still, this conversation didn't make Grace feel as uncomfortable as she'd thought it might. Rather she felt included—part of the club—even if the gist wasn't relevant to her.

While the three women discussed plans for the wedding as well as Taryn's dress, which sounded amazing, Grace spotted Teagan emerging from the house. Looking super-fit in a black and neon-orange tankini, Teagan glanced around. Rising from her chair, Grace excused herself and waved her friend's way.

"What say we fill up some water bombs," Teagan said as Grace moved closer. "We can set off a full-scale attack."

Grace laughed. "You mean against the guys in the pool?"

"Who else?" Teagan took a fruit skewer from the nearby table filled with food. "I still can't believe you're here and Cole's getting married." Teagan's eyes sparkled. "It would be nosey to ask whether you and Wynn are headed that way, wouldn't it? It's just so bizarre thinking of you two together."

Grace's stomach gave a kick. "We're not really together, Tea. Not in the way, say, Shelby is with Dex."

"Oh. Sure." Teagan waved her skewer. "Nothing wrong with cool and casual. Totally understand."

Grace wasn't sure that she did.

She and Teagan hadn't communicated since those pen-pal letters years ago. Even so, Grace now felt that same connection—the trust. It seemed like only yesterday they had shared and talked about everything. Grace wanted to fill her friend in a little on her previous relationship but it wasn't for everyone's ears.

While the others were occupied with wedding talk, she told Teagan about Sam—what a great guy he'd been, how he'd died and how she should have let him go much sooner. She omitted what had transpired thirty minutes before the accident. No one knew the truth about that; she hadn't even written it down in her notebook yet. She finished by saying that whatever she and Wynn shared, it was with a view to having fun in the now rather than till death do them part.

"I'm in a similar kind of relationship," Teagan admitted. "On the surface, we're great together. Underneath, it's complicated."

"Is he coming to the wedding?"

"No. Like I said. Complicated." Teagan slid a grape off

the skewer. "He comes from a big family. His brothers and sisters are all already married. Damon is eager to follow in his siblings' footsteps, which includes heaps of kids."

"How many kids?"

"He's mentioned six."

Grace let out a long whistle. "I was thinking maybe three."

"Maybe none."

Grace's head went back. A couple having a half dozen children wasn't that common nowadays, was it? But none? Was it because Teagan thought it was too soon to be discussing having a family with this man? Maybe his many family members could be nosey and interfering.

Teagan was about to say more when Guthrie and Eloise strolled out of the house. As Guthrie helped his wife into a chair near the pool, Teagan nudged Grace.

"I should go see if they need anything."

Grace was about to follow when a pair of cold, strong arms coiled around her, hauling her back against a hard, equally chilly chest. Yelping, she jumped and tried to spin around, but Wynn wouldn't let go.

"Struggle is futile," he said while his sister laughed.

"Told you," Teagan said. "You should have bombed him while you had the chance."

Two hours later, Tate was in bed and Guthrie stood at the head of the outdoor table, preparing to say a few words. His smile was sincere, but also weary, as if he'd been on a long journey and knew that soon he could rest.

"I don't need to tell anyone how pleased I am to have you all together, to see you happy, particularly, of course, Cole and the soon-to-be bride, our dear Taryn."

While Cole lifted Taryn's hand to his mouth for a kiss, the rest of the gathering put their hands together in a light round of applause.

"Next Sunday will be a special day," Guthrie went on. "I've taken measures to be certain nothing is, well, spoiled." He lowered back into his chair. "Brandon is still working hard to track down information that will lead to the unmasking of the unknown parties who have caused us so much grief these past months. I want you all to be assured that security will be the top priority on the day."

"We've kept the announcement from the press," Cole said. "The invitation list is at bare-bones."

"No red carpet and blowing of horns," Dex pointed out, linking his arm through Shelby's.

"So, who did make the cut?" Teagan asked.

"You guys, of course," Cole said. "Taryn's aunt and a handful of our closest friends."

Wynn remembered Cole mentioning that Taryn's aunt was the only family she had.

"Your Aunt Leeanne and Uncle Stuart." Guthrie began his own list.

"Your sister and her husband? Nice," Teagan said. "We haven't seen them in ages."

"Talbot and Sarah," Guthrie continued, which raised a few eyebrows; until recently, when the attacks had started, the two older Hunter brothers hadn't spoken in years. "And Talbot's son."

Dex sat up. "Slow down. Talbot doesn't have any kids."

Flinching, Eloise pushed lightly on the top of her pregnant belly. "Seems one's worked his way out from the woodwork."

While Guthrie bowed his head as if restraining himself from reacting to the snide remark, Wynn got his mind around the statement—Uncle Talbot had a son? Was he the result of a previous relationship, or had Talbot at some stage strayed from the marriage bed?

Cole's comment was supportive. "I look forward to meeting him."

Guthrie sent a grateful smile. "There are a few people from Hunter Broadcasting. A couple of family friends." He flicked a look Wynn's way before addressing the table again. "Including a longtime friend and his wife, the Riggses."

Wynn sat up. Christopher Riggs's parents? Guess he'd be fielding questions relating to how their boy was doing in New York, not that there was much to report at this early stage.

Dex brought the conversation back to a more serious subject. "So, no new leads on the case?"

"Whoever's responsible," Guthrie said, "seems to have vanished off the face of the earth."

"And hopefully," Eloise added, "that'll be the end of that."

Cole growled. "I won't give up looking for that SOB until he's caught. Neither will Brandon."

Shelby agreed. "If you don't finish it, these kinds of things have an ugly habit of creeping back into your lives." She and Dex shared a look.

Taryn spoke up. "Sometimes troublemakers move to another country. Some simply pass away."

Grace's stomach was knotted as she listened intently to all the back and forths.

If she were Taryn, she would pray for that last scenario. Not only would Taryn want the wedding to unfold without a hitch. She'd want her future children to be immune to these kinds of dangers. All the Hunters wanted to keep Tate free from the possibility of coming to any future harm. One day soon, God willing, Taryn and Cole would have children of their own. Dex and Shelby, too. How could any one of them feel relaxed about having their son or daughter visit this home or spend time with their grandfather with this maniac still on the loose?

Wynn's ex must be grateful she didn't have to deal with

that dilemma. He had said that once he'd wanted to have a family with her. Although now Wynn was steering clear of commitment, which suited this situation just fine.

Wynn reached for her hand.

"You okay?" he said only loud enough for her to hear. The others were still discussing the stalker. "You really don't have to worry," he went on. "I don't know if we'll ever get to the bottom of all this, but those first three incidents were close together. After all this time, I don't think we'll hear from him again."

"So you'd be okay with Tate coming back here to stay?"

Wynn blinked. "He's not my son to say."

"If it were your son," she asked, "what would you do?"

Wynn's jaw tightened as he gave a tight grin. "That's a question I doubt I'll ever need to answer."

Grace watched as a recent-model pickup, boasting the name of a construction firm on its side panel, drove up to the Hunter estate and two privately uniformed men stepped forward to check it at the gate. At the side entrance, which led to the Hunters' vast manicured back lawn, another man waited, constantly running his eye over the zone.

Grace quietly took it all in while waiting for Wynn by their rental car parked on the drive. They'd stayed on for two days, picnicking, boating and generally catching up with his family. She'd been made to feel so welcome; she'd enjoyed every minute, particularly her chance to chill with Teagan, though Tea's idea of relaxation was a ten-mile jog followed by a protein shake. The words cheesecake and alcohol weren't in her vocabulary.

Apparently neither was "kids." Not that Teagan had brought that subject up again.

This morning Wynn had told her it was time to unveil his vacation surprise. They were in for a bit of a drive, he'd explained, but that was all part of the experience.

At breakfast, she and Wynn had said farewell for now to the rest of the clan. A moment ago, packed and about to jump in the car, Wynn had asked if she could wait a second while he gave his little brother another goodbye hug; Guthrie and Cole were in the side yard, teaching Tate to throw a pass.

From the side yard, Taryn spotted her and wandered over.

"The guys are sure enjoying being all together again," Taryn said as she joined her. Wynn had taken the ball and was executing a controlled toss to Tate. Taryn laughed. "You might need to go over and physically drag him away if you want to be on the road by noon."

"I don't mind." Grace straightened her hat; the sun Down Under had a real bite. "This is his time, not mine. I think he misses seeing Tate more than he knows."

"Tate is everyone's favorite, particularly when we all came so close to losing him that day."

Grace shuddered at the thought of seeing a loved one assaulted and then barely escaping an abduction. She couldn't imagine how a child would interpret and internalize all that. As if reading her thoughts, Taryn explained.

"He's spoken with counselors and doesn't appear to have nightmares, thank God. Cole was pretty shaken up over it, though. Not long after that incident, Cole took Tate to a park to toss a ball, like they're doing now. When Cole took his eyes off him for a minute, Tate vanished."

Grace held her sick stomach. "But Cole must have found him."

"Safe and sound. Cole told me later those few moments turned his world upside down. For the first time he understood what he truly wanted from life."

Grace surmised. "A family of his own."

"To protect. To love." Watching her fiancé swing Tate up onto his shoulders, happiness shone in Taryn's eyes.

"Not long after that ordeal, with Brandon Powell on the case, we set sail and got away for a few weeks. That time only brought me and Cole closer together. There hasn't been any trouble since."

"So, maybe Eloise is right," Grace said. "Perhaps the stalker's given up, gone away."

"Doesn't mean the Hunters will give up their search. Whoever's responsible needs to be behind bars."

Eloise appeared in the side yard. Guthrie crossed over to offer a chair to his pregnant wife. Grace couldn't help but notice Cole's reaction to his stepmother's appearance. He seemed to stiffen and his expression cooled before he swung Tate down from his shoulders. When Tate ran to join his mother and father, both Cole and Wynn headed over, too.

Although the men were well out of earshot, Taryn lowered her voice. "I'm sure you've guessed. Eloise isn't Cole's favorite person."

"Wynn mentioned something about how Cole and Dex think she married their father for his money."

"If only that were the worst of it."

Before Taryn could say more, Cole and Wynn were upon them. Cole acknowledged Grace with a big smile before leveling his hands on Taryn's hips and stealing a quick kiss. "What say we see how things are going out back?"

"Sounds good," Taryn replied.

Wynn opened the passenger door of their rental car for Grace. "We'll see you guys in a couple of days."

A moment later, when the convertible passed through the opened gates, both security guards threw them casual salutes. Grace wondered if they were wearing guns, and then whether they would need to use them while they were on this assignment. But everyone seemed so confident. All this security was only a precaution.

Wynn changed gears then reached to hold her hand.

"Ready for an adventure?"
Grace sat straighter and looked ahead.
"Maestro, lead the way."

Nine

By the time they reached the Blue Mountains west of Sydney, Grace had put her questions and concerns regarding the wedding's security out of her mind. Instead, as she slid out of the passenger seat, she focused on the magnificent retreat where Wynn had booked accommodation. With the sash windows and gothic-inspired pointed arches, the hotel reminded her of the Elephant Tea Rooms in London. Then there were the pure, eucalyptus-scented air and serene, top-of-the-world views…

And apparently Wynn had something even more amazing planned.

At the hotel reception counter, a man around Wynn's age lowered his magazine as they approached.

"Morning," the man said. "You have a reservation, sir?"

Wynn gave his name and the man—Mick, according to his badge—studied his computer screen.

"You don't appear to have a booking, Mr. Hunter."

Wynn's eyebrows hiked. "Look again."

A few seconds later, Mick shook his head. "We do have a room available. Ground floor. No view, I'm afraid."

When Wynn's expression hardened and he pulled out his cell phone, Grace cast a look around. A few guests were mulling over brochures. A few more were headed out the door to sight-see, she assumed. She looked back at Mick, who gave her a thin smile before Wynn disconnected. His voice was low and unyielding.

"My assistant assures me a reservation was made. She received a confirmation for a deluxe suite with views. She spoke with you personally, Mick."

Rubbing a palm over his shirt, Mick analyzed the screen again, and then his shoulders bounced with a "can't help you" shrug. "I apologize, sir."

Wynn rapped a set of fingertips on the counter. "Is your manager in?"

A little girl, around April's age, had wandered out from a room adjoining the reception area. She tugged on Mick's sleeve. "Daddy, wanna help me color?"

Mick called the manager before combing a palm over his daughter's wispy fair hair. "Hang on, peaches."

After a three-hour drive, Grace was simply happy to be here. She didn't care what kind of room they had. She certainly didn't want to upset that little girl.

Setting a forearm on the counter, Mick leaned closer. "I can do a great deal on that room, but all the suites are taken."

Another man strolled out. Introducing himself as the manager, he enquired, "Is there a problem?"

As Mick explained and Wynn put his objection forward, Grace stepped back. The manager was apologetic. Then, when he realized who Wynn was—the Hunter family was legendary in Australia—he was doubly so. When Mick got tongue-tied—he couldn't explain the missing email or botched booking—the little girl crept back and hid behind that door. Her chocolate-brown eyes were wide. She had no idea what the problem was, why her daddy was upset.

Wynn saw her too and held up his hands. "Don't worry," he said. "We'll take that room."

"I'm so sorry, Mr. Hunter," the manager said again.

Wynn took the key card. When they reached their compact double room on the ground floor, Grace was curious.

Wynn dropped his cell phone on a table. "Not what I had in mind."

"You weren't happy."

"I'm not a fan of incompetence."

"You wanted to tell them both that."

"I think I had a right."

"But you didn't." She moved over. "Why not?"

He shrugged. "No point."

"It was because of that little girl, wasn't it? You saw her watching so you dropped it."

"It wasn't that big of a deal, Grace."

Grinning, she trailed a fingertip around his scratchy jaw. "You backed off."

He narrowed his eyes at her. "You like a man who backs down?"

"For those kinds of reasons, absolutely." She circled her finger around the warm hollow at the base of his throat. "You can be quite chivalrous, do you know that?"

"As opposed to what you thought of me as a kid." His hands skimmed down her sides. "You didn't think that I was behaving in a gentlemanly fashion back then, remember?"

"Except whenever I teased you, no matter how much you wanted to belt me, you always walked away."

His lips twitched as he moved in closer. "I remember at least one time when Cole needed to hold me back."

Standing on her toes, she brushed the tip of her nose against his. "Face it, Wynn Hunter. You're one of the good guys."

"Uh-uh." He angled his head to nip her lower lip. "I'm bad to the bone."

Before she let him kiss her, she admitted, "But in a very good way."

Two hours later, Grace was gazing upon the most incredible site she could ever have imagined. And this place was used for wedding ceremonies? *Wow.*

Wynn had bought tickets for a tour of the Lucas Cave, the most popular of the three hundred forty million-year-old Jenolan Caves, which were within walking distance of the hotel. After climbing hundreds of steps, they entered an anteroom and then the Cathedral Chamber, which soared to a staggering fifty-four meters at its highest point. It reminded her of that scene out of *The Adventures of Tom Sawyer.*

Grace instantly forgot the muscle burn from the climb as she stood in the midst of such amazing limestone formations. Some looked like stained glass windows. The guide pointed out a limestone bell tower and a pulpit, too.

The chamber could accommodate up to one hundred guests and the acoustics were apparently perfect; orchestras and a local Aboriginal band regularly entertained audiences here. When the guide wanted to show how disorientating the caves could become without electricity, she turned out the lights. As they were dropped into darkness, Grace gripped Wynn's arm while he chuckled and held her tight.

Farther along the flights of narrow stairs that wove through the caverns, the temperature dropped and they were introduced to formations that looked like sheets of white lace, as well as ribbons of stalactites that flared with reddish-orange hues. In another cave, pure white calcite formations looked like icicles dripping from the ceiling and snow-dusted firs sprouting up from the ground.

When they emerged from the cave and were greeted by

warm sunshine again, they walked hand in hand around the fern-bordered Blue Lake, which was, indeed, a heavenly, untouched deep blue. They spotted a platypus; Grace stood spellbound as the mammal, which looked like a cross between a duck and an otter, wiggled around the bank, foraging for food. As they approached a group of wallabies, she expected them all to hop away. One actually let her brush a palm over its supersoft fur and look into those liquid black eyes. Later, however, she was more than a little hesitant, skirting around the frozen, guarded posture of a dragon lizard.

She flicked on her phone's camera, snapped a few shots of the wildlife and sent them straight through to April via her mom's cell. Grace got a reply back a minute later. April wanted to know if her auntie could bring home a wallaby.

Back at the hotel, she and Wynn showered and changed for dinner at a nearby first-class restaurant. Thankfully there weren't any hiccups with reservations this time.

They were halfway through their meal when conversation turned to work. Wynn had asked about her studies.

"Before getting my masters," she said, "I had dreams of starting my own practice."

"What does a person need to study to get a license for speech therapy?"

"Speech-language pathology. I learned about anatomy, physiology, the development of the areas of the body involved in language, speech and swallowing."

"Did you say swallowing?"

"People don't tend to realize how important it is."

He grinned. "I've always been a fan."

Setting down his cutlery, Wynn reached for his glass. He'd chosen a wine produced in Victoria—an exquisite light white. After forking more of the creamy scalloped potato into her mouth, Grace picked up the thread of their conversation.

"We studied the nature of disorders, acoustics, as well as the psychological side of things. Then we explored how to evaluate and treat problems."

"I knew a boy who stuttered. Aaron Fenway could barely get his name out. It must have been tough. But it didn't seem to faze him. He was always top of the class at math."

"Sounds like my younger sister. A head for figures."

"Aaron owns a huge dot-com now."

"Bruce Willis and Nicole Kidman stuttered. Winston Churchill and Shaquille O'Neal, too."

"I'm trying to imagine anyone being brave enough to tease Shaquille."

"Apparently, when Shaquille was a kid, he'd sit in class, sweating over whether the teacher would ask him a question. He knew he wouldn't be able to get the words out."

"Must make you feel good, helping." Wynn set down his glass. "The business I'm in doesn't have that kind of reputation, I'm afraid."

"News needs to be told. It's a noble profession."

"It can be. Lots of challenges ahead of us there, though. More and more readers are getting their news off the Net."

"So, what's the future?"

"Keep our eyes open to all the options. Change is the one constant. We need to look at cutting costs on the print side. Factory and distribution overheads. I'm talking with someone at the moment."

"To share those costs?"

"More than that. We're looking to merge parts of our companies."

"Ooh, sounds very highflier."

"And very confidential. Not even my father knows."

She studied his expression and put down her fork. "You don't look as if you're punching the air about telling him."

"Guthrie's idea of building success is to buy out the opposition or run them out of business. He doesn't *merge*."

"Isn't that your decision? You run Hunter Publishing now."

"For things to go smoothly, I need his approval." He pushed his plate aside. "And I need it soon. Better to explain face-to-face."

"Sometime this week?" He nodded. "Maybe keep it for after the wedding."

"My thoughts exactly."

After the meal, the young waitress served coffee and asked if they'd enjoyed the tours.

"I saw you this afternoon," the waitress explained, "wandering back from the Grand Arch."

Grace well remembered the Arch. According to the guide, while that particular cave had collapsed many centuries ago, the giant rock arch of the original structure remained—a truly awe-inspiring sight.

Grace sighed. "It was all amazing."

"Did anyone mention the ghosts?" the waitress asked, setting down the cups.

Wynn's lips twitched. "We missed that tour."

But Grace remembered seeing a mysteries and ghosts tour outlined on a brochure.

"There's evidence of strange things happening down there—photographs and videos." The waitress lowered her voice. "There's even supposed to be a ghost living right here, in this restaurant."

"Does she float around the town, as well," Wynn asked, "rattling her teapot?"

"If she does," the waitress said, "don't worry. She's friendly."

Later, when Grace and Wynn were back at their hotel and entering their room, Wynn suddenly grabbed her from behind, around the waist. Grace's heart leapt to the ceiling before, spinning around, she smacked his shoulder and, heart pounding, turned on the lights. Why did guys think stuff like that was funny? It wasn't—or at least not when she'd imagined the sound of footfalls following them up the street. She might have heard a teapot rattle, too.

"You're such a child."

He laughed as she strode off. "Oh, *I'm* a child? Will we leave on a night-light tonight?"

"I'd love to see how smart you'd be if a ghost sailed through that door right now and poured cold tea all over your head."

He followed her. "So you believe all that haunted house woo-ha." Lashing an arm around her middle, he growled against her lips, "Good thing I'm here to protect you."

Refusing to grin, she set her palms on his chest, which seemed to have grown harder and broader since the last time they'd made this kind of contact.

"I have an open mind. I can also look after myself."

"Just letting you know," he said, lowering his head to nuzzle her neck, "I'm here if you need me." He nuzzled lower. "For anything." His hand curved over her behind. "Anything at all."

Her eyes had drifted shut. Damn the man. She couldn't stay mad.

"You want to help?" she asked.

"Want me to order a medium? Organize a séance? Sprinkle some salt on the threshold?"

She grabbed his shirt and tugged him toward the cozy double bed. "You're going to help me with a whole lot more than that."

Ten

"**P**romise me one thing," Grace said.

Wynn squeezed her hand. "Anything?"

"No stunt today like the one you pulled at that other wedding."

When she and Wynn had returned from their magical stay at the Blue Mountains with a hundred snaps and a thousand memories, the final preparations for Cole and Taryn's big day were in full swing. They'd watched the extensive back lawn and gardens being pruned to perfection. A giant fairy-tale marquee had shot up and the furnishings had been arranged both inside and out.

Now Grace looked around at the marquee's ceiling draped with white silk swags and the fountains of flowers, as the sixty or so guests took their seats on either side of a red-carpeted aisle.

Beside her, Wynn wore a tuxedo in a way that would impress James Bond. Now, responding to her request that he behave himself, he sent her a wicked grin and stage whispered, "No surprise kiss in front of the multitudes? Why? Can't handle it?"

She tugged his ear. "Mister, I can handle anything you care to dish out."

"Except letting people know that there might be more."

"More of what?"

"More to us."

That took her aback. What did he mean *more*? They were here in Australia, doing exactly as he'd suggested: relaxing and enjoying themselves. There wasn't any *more* to it.

Or she was reading too much into his words. That tease was more likely a warning that she shouldn't become too complacent. He just might shock the crowd again. She had news for him.

"Just remember whose show this is, okay?"

"Yep." The corners of his smoldering eyes crinkled. "Can't handle it."

When he leaned closer, she put on a business-only face and dusted imaginary lint from his broad shoulders. "Time you went and joined your brothers at the altar."

He gave her a curious look. "You think so?"

She hesitated before laughing. He was acting so strangely today.

"You look amazing in that dress," he said.

"You told me," she grinned. "Maybe ten times."

He tipped close and took a light but lingering kiss that brought a mist to her eyes. His warm palm curved around her cheek. "You'll be here when I get back?"

She wanted to laugh again, but his gaze was suddenly so serious.

"Yes," she said and softly smiled. "I'll be right here. I promise."

On Wynn's way to the platform where Cole and Dex waited, Guthrie pulled him aside to introduce a couple who seemed familiar, in more ways than one.

"Son, you remember Vincent and Kirsty Riggs," Guthrie said with his father-of-the-groom smile firmly in place.

"Of course." Wynn shook Vincent's hand and nodded a greeting at the wife. "Nice to see you both again."

Mr. Riggs's expression was humble. "Christopher's so pleased that you've allowed him this chance in New York."

"I'm sure he'll be an asset to the company," Wynn replied.

"We should catch up after the ceremony," Vincent went on. "I'd like to know what you have in store for him."

"But right now," Mrs. Riggs said, nodding at the altar, "you have an important job to do."

"Guthrie mentioned that Dex will be joining his older brother soon," Vincent said, "tying the knot."

When Vincent flicked a glance Grace's way and waited for some kind of response, Wynn only grinned and replied, "It's true. Dex will soon be a married man. Another reason to celebrate." Wynn bowed off. "Please excuse me."

Strolling up to the platform, Wynn concentrated on the task ahead. He and Dex were to stand beside the oldest Hunter brother as he took this important step in his life. But another related thought kept knocking around in his brain.

After that initial hiccup with their booking, he and Grace had enjoyed every second of their time away in the mountains. They'd explored, eaten out, talked a lot and when they weren't otherwise engaged, made love. He had assumed the constant physical desire would, in some way, slack off. Anything but. His need to feel her curled up around him, have his mouth working together with hers, had been a constant. He understood sexual attraction, but he and Grace seemed to have created their own higher meaning.

Ever since he'd been here, when he and Cole and Dex sat down at the end of the day with a beer, he listened to their banter about how much they looked forward to settling down, and the ache he'd suffered after that bust-up with Heather had begun to fester again. In the past, whenever he'd looked ahead, Heather had been there, standing alongside him. But seeing Grace tonight in that knockout strapless red gown with the sweetest of all sweetheart necklines, silver bangles jangling on both wrists and her eyes filled with sass and life...

He didn't want a relationship, and yet he and Grace were doing a darn fine imitation of having one. A moment ago, after he'd hinted at perhaps wanting more, for just a second, he'd meant it. But he didn't need to go down that track again. Why rock a perfectly happy boat?

He was nearing the platform when another guest stopped him—a tall, well-built man in his twenties.

"You're Wynn, right?" the man asked.

"We've met?"

"I'm Sebastian Styles."

Wynn thought back and then apologized. "No light bulb, I'm afraid."

"Talbot's son."

Wynn had known to expect his long-lost cousin today, but no one had passed on a name. And while the brothers had speculated, no one seemed to know the story behind this surprise addition to the Hunter line. Which wasn't a problem. Sebastian Styles was family now and more than welcome.

As the men shook hands, Wynn confirmed, "Good to meet you."

"I wasn't sure whether Guthrie had explained my sudden arrival on the scene."

"Only that you'd caught up with your father."

The rest really wasn't any of Wynn's business. He glanced toward the platform—he needed to take his place alongside his brothers right now.

"I've heard plenty about you," Sebastian was saying,

"and your brothers. Can I join you for a drink after the ceremony?"

"I look forward to it."

Wynn skirted around the front section of chairs, which were filling with guests, and came to stand alongside Dex—three Hunter brothers all in a row.

Assuming the apparently obligatory "hands clasped in front" stance, he asked the others, "We set to go?"

Dex dug into a breast pocket and flicked out a clean white handkerchief for Cole. "For when the perspiration starts coursing down your face."

"I'm not nervous." Cole straightened his bow tie. "This is the best day of my life."

"When you know it's right, you know," Dex said, and the two older brothers bumped shoulders before remembering themselves. They were happy, settled. Wynn was not.

Oh, for pity's sake.

"I wish you two would stop going all goofy on me," Wynn growled. "I thought you'd know by now—I'm over that other stuff."

"Grace is a special woman," Cole said sagely.

Dex followed up with, "You two give off some pretty intense sparks. As long as you're both having fun. Right, Cole?"

But Cole's attention was elsewhere. He straightened his tie again.

"My master of ceremonies just gave the signal. Taryn's ready to come out." Cole sent his brothers a fortifying wink. "See you on the other side, boys."

Grace was figuring out the seating arrangements.

The only person she recognized in the first row, which was set aside for family, was a put-upon Eloise, who was draped in yellow chiffon and nursing a baby bump that looked more like a balloon ready to pop. Teagan was a bridesmaid and Tate, a page boy. Shelby wasn't anywhere to be seen. Without Wynn to sit beside, Grace didn't want to crash. Perhaps she ought to sit more toward the middle—neutral territory.

She was deciding on a row when, looking breathtaking in a glamorous single-shoulder, emerald-green gown, Shelby came rushing up.

"You're sitting with me," she said, indicating the second row before continuing on her way. "I'll be back in a shake. Just want to give one of the best men a big kiss for good luck."

Lowering onto the outermost chair of the row Shelby had indicated, Grace was perusing the leather-bound order of service when a man appeared at her side—the man Grace had seen Wynn speak with before taking his place beside his brothers on the platform.

"Is there room for one more?" the man asked.

He had a presence about him, Grace decided, which complemented his smooth baritone and kind hazel-colored eyes.

"Of course." Grace moved over.

Settling in, the man rubbed both palms down his suit's thighs before he glanced at her. "I'm feeling a little out of the circle."

She returned his awkward smile. "Me, too."

"I'm Sebastian Styles, by the way. The long-lost cousin."

"Grace Munroe." She added, "Third brother's date."

"I didn't feel as if I should intrude today. It's such a private affair. Smaller guest list than I'd even imagined."

It wasn't her place to ask how much Sebastian knew about the stalker business, so she merely agreed with his last point.

"At first, I declined the invite," Sebastian said. "But Talbot and, apparently, Guthrie insisted."

She nodded toward a couple in the front row. "Are they your parents?"

"That's Leeanne—Talbot and Guthrie's sister—and her husband, Stuart Somersby. Sitting alongside them are Josh and Naomi, their grown kids."

From this vantage point, Josh looked to be in his early twenties with sandy-colored hair and strong Hunter features, including a hawkish nose. Biting her lip she was so excited, Naomi was younger and extremely attractive. Her tumble of pale blond hair was dotted with diamantés.

Perhaps having heard her name, Leeanne—a slender, stylish brunette—glanced over her shoulder and wiggled her fingers, *hi*. Sebastian and Grace wiggled back before he nodded toward a magnificent display of flowers where two men were discussing some obviously serious matter.

"That's Talbot, my father, speaking with Guthrie."

"Neither one looks happy."

"I'm guessing it's about the security. My father was none too pleased about being frisked so thoroughly at the door." Sebastian's brow creased before he hung his head and smiled. "My father. Still sounds weird."

"I know everyone's looking forward to meeting you." She turned a little toward him. "Do you have a partner?"

His expression changed before he straightened in his seat. "No. Nothing like that."

The music morphed into a moving tune that Cole and Taryn had chosen to kick off this all-important part of the day. When the bride appeared, on the arm of the woman who must be her Aunt Vi, a rush of happy tears sprang to Grace's eyes. Who didn't love a wedding?

Shelby appeared and Sebastian and Grace both shifted one seat over in the row.

Pressing a palm to her heart, Shelby whispered to them both. "What a gorgeous dress. She's the most beautiful bride I've ever seen."

Then Tate, in a tiny tux, and Teagan and another bridesmaid started off down the aisle and Grace sat back.

This was bound to be an amazing day.

Hours after the ceremony, during the reception that was
also held inside the marquee, Grace caught a glimpse of
Teagan. She stood behind a massive, decorative column,
a cell phone pressed to her ear. Biting a nail, she looked
upset enough to cry.

The music filtered through the sound system, drawing
lots of couples onto the dance floor. Grace had just finished
speaking with a couple—Christopher Riggs's parents, as
a matter of fact—lovely people who seemed pleased their
son was moving forward with his life in New York.

Grace had been ready to join Wynn, who appeared to
be enjoying his conversation with his new cousin. Now,
Grace hurried over to Teagan.

"You're upset," she said as Teagan disconnected her call.

"That guy I've been telling you about…" Teagan tacked
up a weak smile. "He's missing me."

Grace let out a sigh of relief. That wasn't bad. That was
sweet. Grace had wanted to learn more about Teagan's guy
but when her friend hadn't brought the subject up again,
Grace didn't want to prod.

Now she said, "Looks like you're missing him, too."

Beneath the marquee's slow-spinning lights, Teagan's
gaze grew distant and her jaw tensed, as if she were trying to keep from frowning.

"Guess I've gotten used to having him around. Except…
I can't see things working out between us. Not in the long
term."

"Because he wants lots of children?"

Teagan nodded.

Teagan's guy sounded a lot like Sam, Grace thought.

Difference was that Teagan obviously cared deeply for this man in the way a future wife should.

"So, he's proposed?" Grace asked.

"Not yet. And I don't want him to. Like I said, it's complicated. I was going to talk with you more about it, but…"

"You don't have to explain—"

"I want to." She took Grace's champagne flute and downed half the glass—a big deal, given that Teagan didn't usually drink.

After a visible shudder, Teagan handed the glass back. "That accident I had all those years ago…"

They'd spoken about that, too, these past days. "You were in and out of hospital."

"I missed so much school. Mom and Dad tried to make it up to me. I had every material thing a girl would wish for. I think they knew pretty much from the start. I found out later." Her lips pressed together and, staring off at the people dancing, she blinked several times. "I can't have children."

The words hung in the air between them before Grace's heart sank to her knees. She gripped her friend's hand. She'd never dream for one minute…

"Oh, Tea…"

"It's okay," she said quickly. "I'm used to the idea. There's plenty of other things in life to keep a person focused and busy."

"Maybe if you spoke to him. There are options."

"Sure. Great ones. But you'd have to meet him, Grace. I look at him and know he's destined to have boys with his strong chin and the same sparkling blue eyes." Her wistful expression hardened. "He deserves everything he wants from life."

"Speak with him," Grace implored.

Teagan's chin lifted even as she smiled. "I'm fine with who I am. I don't want anyone's pity. I've had enough of that in my life. I certainly don't want to put him in a position where he feels he has to choose."

Between marrying the woman he loved and marrying someone else who could bear his children?

Grace remembered those hours she and Teagan had spent as kids playing with baby dolls, pretending to feed and rock and diaper change. Grace took for granted that when she was happily settled and tried to get pregnant, she wouldn't have trouble. Of course, adoption and surrogates had proven wonderful alternatives for so many couples who couldn't conceive. Although Teagan said she was used to the idea of being unable to conceive, something in her eyes said that this minute, she found acceptance hard.

When the music faded, both women's attentions were drawn by some commotion playing out on the marquee's platform. Taryn was getting ready to toss her bouquet. So Grace put her conversation with Teagan aside. If her friend ever wanted to talk more, Grace would be available, even from halfway around the world.

Having composed herself, Teagan tipped her head toward the gathering and put on a brave face. "Are you having a go?"

"Last time I was involved with a bouquet, I got way more than I bargained for."

Teagan grinned. Grace had told her about that kiss at the reception.

"I'm rooting for Shelby," Teagan said. "But I'll help make up the numbers."

When Teagan and the other eligible women were positioned on the dance floor, Taryn spun around and then threw her bouquet. The flowers sailed a few yards before Shelby, using her height advantage, snatched them out of the air. As people cheered, Dex marched up to her. Pride shining from his face, he dipped his fiancée in a dramatic pose before kissing her. All the wedding crowd sighed, including Grace.

Those two seemed so right for each other. It was as if all their edges and emotions were two halves of a whole.

At first, Grace had been hesitant about coming to Australia, to this event. She'd worried she might need to defend the fact that she and Wynn weren't serious the way Cole and Taryn were. The way people had assumed she and Sam had been.

And yet, with all these sentimental feelings surrounding her now, Grace felt as if she were falling into that very trap herself. In these couple of weeks, she felt so connected to Wynn.

From the platform, the DJ asked the women to move aside. Cole was preparing to throw the bride's garter.

Wynn stood at the back of the pack. When he caught sight of her, he sent over a wave an instant before Dex grabbed both his brother's arms and, fooling around, struggled to hold them behind Wynn's back. Grace laughed even as her chest tightened. Like the bouquet, tradition said that the person who caught the garter was meant to marry next. Dex would want to catch the garter and slip it on his fiancée's leg. But, as he wrangled free of Dex's hold and prepared to leap, Wynn seemed just as determined. A competitive spirit.

Or something more?

Teagan joined her. No one would guess that she'd been close to tears a few minutes ago.

"Look at those brothers of mine." When Dex tried to body block Wynn, Wynn elbowed his way in front again and Teagan laughed. "I've never seen Wynn have so much fun as he has this trip. These past months, whenever we've spoken on the phone, he's been so distant." Teagan wound her arm through Grace's. "Then you came along."

Grace looked at her twice. Right there was the kind of

comment she hadn't wanted to deal with during this trip. Wynn had lost the woman he had wanted to marry. Grace hadn't wanted to come across as anyone's replacement. She was still working through her own past.

And yet, something inside her had shifted. Something had changed.

Up on the stage, the groom knelt before his new bride and slipped the garter off her leg. As he held it above his head, the bullpen erupted with calls to begin.

The DJ revved them up more. "Guys, are you ready?"

A roar went up, the groom about-faced, and then the garter went flying at the same time as Wynn's heels grew wings. He caught the garter on a single finger. Feet back on the ground, he accepted slaps on the back from his peers. Meanwhile, out of the corner of her eye, she noticed Tate scooting through the pack and climbing the steps to the platform. He'd been having a blast dancing up there most of the night.

Wynn ambled over to her and dropped to one knee. The room hushed and all eyes fell upon them. Grace shrank back. This all had a familiar ring to it.

"Heel up here," Wynn demanded and slapped his raised thigh.

And have everyone ask later whether they'd set a date? That was going too far. She shook her head.

He sent her a devilish smile. "Guess I could always wear it as a headband." When he widened the garter and threatened to fit it around his crown, the crowd exploded with laughter. "You can't disappoint everyone." His voice lowered and gaze deepened. "Don't disappoint me."

The DJ stepped in, egging her on, and the crowd got on board. Wynn's expression wasn't teasing now. It was… solemn.

Grace's heart was booming in her chest, in her ears. This display was sending the wrong message.

Or was it just a bit of fun? With all the room smiling at them, she couldn't help but smile herself.

She placed one shoe on his knee. He slipped the garter up over her toes to just above the knee and then, holding her gaze with his, pushed to his feet. Rather than applaud, their audience was hushed. Were the guests aware of the energy pulsating between the two of them?

"Know what this calls for?" he asked.

She felt almost giddy. "A modest bow?"

Of course, his arms wound around her, and when his lips touched hers, any urge she might have had to push away, tell him to behave, faded into longing. She hadn't wanted to be the center of attention. She didn't want people to peg her into yet another hole. And yet...

Sensations gathered, vibrating through her body and spilling out like ripples from the sweetest sounding bell. For the slightest fragment in time, she believed that the fireworks going off in her mind and through her blood were so powerful that they physically shook the room.

Then a different reality struck, and the crowd began to scream.

Eleven

The force from the blast almost knocked Wynn over.

With the noise from the explosion ringing in his ears, he spun around. A piece of debris smacked his cheek as a haze of dark smoke erupted from somewhere near the platform. He remembered who had been standing there a second earlier and his stomach crashed to his knees.

He turned to Grace. "Get out of here. *Run!*"

With a hacking cough, she gripped his arm. "Tate's over there."

He knew it. He spun her around.

"Go!"

He headed toward the smoke by the platform, at the same time checking out the rest of the area. Guests smeared with dust and debris were charging toward the exit. He couldn't see Cole or Dex but, glancing over his shoulder, he caught sight of Taryn and Shelby helping Grace outside. Chances were his brothers were somewhere searching in this smoke, too.

With sparks spitting against his face, his nostrils burning and surrounded by the smell of his own singed hair, he leapt onto the platform. A pint-size silhouette—Tate?—stood frozen off to one side. If he'd been knocked down, he was on his feet again now. He'd be disorientated, possibly injured.

Wynn was bolting across when another explosion went off—different from the first. It was the electrical equipment shorting. Catching fire. Flames spewed out from the area where the DJ had set up. Heat radiated from the fire, searing Wynn's back as Tate's smudged, frightened face appeared in the smoke. His little hands were covering his ears. His eyes were clamped shut. Lunging, Wynn heaved Tate up against his chest, holding him close with one arm.

He was jumping off the creaking platform when Brandon materialized out of the chaos, holding an extinguisher. Brandon acknowledged Tate before disappearing back into the haze.

A moment later, Wynn was out in the sunshine, legs pumping toward the house where many of the startled guests had gathered. Security men were herding them back. Teagan was on her cell, presumably to emergency services, although he was certain one of Brandon's men would have sent up the alarm already. Teagan was also consoling Eloise, who was visibly shaken. When Teagan saw Tate, she covered her mouth to catch a gasp of relief. Dropping her phone, she put out her arms.

As Wynn passed the boy over, he did a quick check. Tate's little dress shirt was gray from the smoke, but Wynn didn't see any blood. The child's eyes were still closed, his face slack. Poor kid must have fainted.

While Teagan cradled Tate, Eloise seemed to emerge from her stupor. She brought both Teagan and Tate close, hugging them as much as her belly would allow. Wynn spun away, searching for Grace. And then, familiar arms were around him and she was saying, "Thank God you're out. Thank God you're safe."

He pulled her back, looked into her eyes. Grace was shaken but unhurt.

The screams of sirens bled in over the noise of the fire that had eaten through the marquee's ceiling. He gripped her arms. "I'm going back in."

As he pulled away, she tried to hold him back. Her eyes were as wide as saucers. They said, *Please, please, don't go.* During that beat in time, he remembered her ex had been a firefighter; if he had died in an accident, Wynn guessed it had been a blaze. But today he had no choice.

He couldn't see his father anywhere. Cole and Dex must be inside that trap, too. Engines were on their way, but there were extinguishers in there; Brandon had gone through safety procedures thoroughly with them before the guests had arrived and now his team needed help.

As Wynn sprinted back through the entrance, shock subsided into rage. When they found whoever was responsible, he wanted just five minutes alone with the son of a bitch. He wanted a fight?

This meant war.

"This time yesterday, champagne corks were flying down there." Grace turned from the window as Wynn entered the bedroom. "Hard to believe it's all cordoned off now with police tape."

Brandon Powell and his team, along with Wynn and his brothers, had extinguished the majority of flames before emergency services had arrived. Consequently, most of the marquee still stood, but the air outside reeked with the stench of charred debris. As Wynn joined her, Grace turned again to the view. This side of the crime scene tape, Brandon stood, arms crossed, as he spoke with a detective. A few feet away from them lay a bunch of flowers—Taryn's bouquet?—dirty and trampled.

"Teagan's with Tate." Wynn's arms wound around her middle as he pressed his chest snug against her back. "I can't believe he came out of it all with nothing more than a couple of scratches." He rested his chin on her crown. "He can't remember anything between the time I caught the garter and when he came to outside."

"Will he ever remember?"

"No one knows."

Hearing the screams and feeling the heat of the flames again, Grace winced and, pressing back against Wynn more, hugged his arms all the tighter. She hoped Tate never remembered.

Wynn turned her around to face him. "Cole followed up on his guests. Other than still being a little shell-shocked, everyone's fine."

"I guess the authorities will be in touch with them all."

"Brandon, too. If anyone saw anything that didn't fit, it'll come out. No one's going to let up until we track down whoever's responsible. In the meantime, Dad's been offered protective custody. He's considering it."

The Hunter clan had spent the night in a nearby hotel with security. After the grounds and house had been swept by the bomb team and cleared, they'd returned this morning. But questions remained: Would that madman try to strike again here? When? How?

The public was curious, too.

"Is the media still out front?" she asked.

"It's news," he groaned, before leading her to the bed and coaxing her to lie down next to him. Studying her expression, he brushed some hair away from her cheek.

"Did you get ahold of your family?" he asked.

"Mom says she wants me back right away."

"I'll speak with your father myself. Pass on my apologies."

"This isn't your fault."

"I'm still responsible. Cole doesn't want Taryn anywhere near this place. He's stepped up the security at the Hunter Broadcasting building, too."

"And Dex?"

"He wants Tate to go back to L.A. with him and Shelby. Makes sense, but Tate is clinging to his mom." He cursed. "Christ, this is a mess."

"And you?"

He held her chin and told her firmly, "I agree with your mother. I need to get you out of here."

He brushed his lips over hers and it didn't matter what had gone before—she felt nothing but safe.

"Did you get an update from Brandon?" she asked.

"He's adamant that every workman and hospitality person was checked coming in and going out. They've bagged some evidence that'll help determine the sophistication of the device, although bets are it was small and crude. No suspicion of high-grade explosive material."

He pressed a soft kiss to her brow. The warm tingles fell away as he pushed up off the bed and onto his feet.

"We have seats booked on an evening flight to New York," he said, moving to pour a glass of water from a carafe. "And you'll be flying on to Florida a few days after that."

It was a statement. And she did need to get back to Florida. She'd just expected to be here a couple more days. It was all ending so quickly.

"I've told Teagan we need to keep in touch," she said. "Either she'll come out to the East Coast or I'll visit her in Seattle."

He moved to the window to gaze out over the debris in silence.

She swung her feet over the edge of the mattress onto the floor. If she was ever going to know, she might as well ask now.

"What was she like?"

"What was who like?"

"The woman in that hotel foyer that night." *The woman you used to love. Perhaps still love.* "What was her name?"

When he faced her, his jaw was tight. She thought he was going to say he didn't want to talk about her, not ever. But then his chin lifted and clearly, calmly, he said, "Her name is Heather Matthews."

Grace crossed over to join him at the window. "I met Sam at a local baseball game. I dropped my hot dog. He offered to buy me another one."

Wynn considered her for a long moment.

"I met Heather at a gallery opening. She's a photographer. Inventive. Artistic. My perfect foil." He frowned to himself. "That's what I'd thought."

"Sam asked for my number," she said. "He asked me out the next week. A movie and hamburger afterward. Not long after that, I met his parents and he met mine."

"Cole and Dex were the devout bachelors," he said. "Too busy with other things to worry about that kind of commitment. But me…"

"You proposed."

"After two years."

"Sam and I were together for five years before…"

"He asked you to be his wife. And you said yes."

They were talking so openly, feeding off each other's stories. Now she opened her mouth to correct him. She hadn't accepted Sam's proposal. She'd turned him down. But the words stuck in her throat. If she admitted that— told him the truth about that, wouldn't he view her as another Heather? A woman who gave a man in love some hope only to wrench it away.

What would he think about her if he knew the rest of the story?

He set his glass on the window ledge and held her. "I didn't lose what you lost. *How* you lost."

Her stomach turned over. If he only knew…

"It was hard for you, too. Although…" She said the rest before she could stop herself. "Heather was only being honest with you."

He cocked his head as his mouth twisted into an uncertain grin. "Are you defending her?"

Grace was defending herself.

"The truth is," he said, "that when we met, I had industry connections. Two years on, she didn't need them anymore."

The urge swelled up inside Grace like a big bubble of hot air. She had to be honest with him, even if he could never understand.

"Wynn, I need to tell you something."

His face warmed with a smile that she imagined he kept only for her. "You don't need to tell me anything."

"I do."

"If it's something more about Sam, you don't have to explain. That explosion, those flames—yesterday would have shaken you up maybe more than any of us. I was cut when Heather and I broke up, but I didn't lose her in a fire—"

"Wynn, Sam didn't die in a fire."

His brows snapped together. "He was a firefighter." She nodded. "When your father mentioned an accident, I assumed…"

"Sam died in a car crash."

She wanted to tell him more, tell him everything, how she'd felt about Sam, how the years they'd spent together as a couple had just seemed to pass and drift by. She wanted to tell him about the secret that she had yet to describe even in that notebook. But now she couldn't bear to think of how quickly that thoughtful look Wynn was sharing with her now would turn into a sneer.

He led her over to a sofa. They sat together, his arm around her, her cheek resting against his chest. After a time, he dropped a kiss on her brow and asked, "Will you be okay alone for a while? I need to speak with my father. I need to get something off my chest before we leave."

"About that merger deal?" she asked.

"I'm not looking forward to it. Especially not after yesterday."

She held his hand. "You'll still be his son."

He sent her a crooked grin. "Fingers crossed."

Wynn found Eloise reclining on a chaise lounge, lamenting over the images in a swimwear catalogue. Seeing him, she seemed to deflate even more.

"Honey, could you bring me some ice tea from the bar?" She fanned herself with the catalogue. "I feel so parched. Must be all that ash floatin' around."

Wynn dropped some ice in a highball glass and then filled it from a pitcher in the bar fridge. Handing it over, he asked, "Where's Dad?"

"In his study, last I heard, worrying over insurance."

Soon, he'd be worrying about even more than that.

Wynn turned to leave, but Eloise called him back. She had a certain look on her face. He thought it might be sincerity.

"Wynn, I need to thank you."

Was this about how he'd rescued Tate from the burning marquee? He waved it off. "You've already done that."

Everybody had, but no one needed to. In his place, anyone would have done the same.

Eloise dragged herself to a sitting position. "I want to thank you for supporting us—my family. Supporting *me*."

Her chin went down and her gaze dropped. "I'm ashamed to say, I haven't always deserved it."

"There's no need to—"

"No. There is." Her palm caressed her big belly. "I may not be a fairy-tale mother, but I do love Tate. With him being away so much this year, with us almost losing him yesterday…" Her eyes glistened and her mouth formed what Wynn knew was a genuine smile. "I don't know what I'd do without you all."

Wynn allowed a smile of his own before he headed out. In a place he rarely visited, he knew the truth: some time ago, Eloise had propositioned Cole. Before this stalker trouble had begun, Tate had lived here in Sydney. Cole had had the benefit of seeing their father and Tate regularly, but he also had to contend with those issues surrounding his stepmother. Not pleasant.

Wynn arrived at his father's study and knocked on the door. He waited before knocking again. When there was no response, he opened the door and edged inside. Guthrie sat in a corner, staring into space. His hair looked grayer and thinner. The frustration and despair showed in every line on his face. As Wynn drew nearer, his father roused himself—even tried to paste on a smile.

"Take a seat, son."

"I wanted to let you know," Wynn began, "Grace and I are flying out this evening."

"Understood. Only sensible."

"If there's anything I can do… If you need me to come back for any reason—"

"You need to get back to New York. They'll be missing you there."

Wynn rubbed the scar on his temple. "There's a lot going on. Lots of industry changes."

"How do they put it? The death of print. We simply need

to find ways to work around it. Diversify. Make sure we're the last man standing."

"Actually, I have something in the pipeline. Something I'm afraid you won't like."

A keen look flashed in his father's eyes. "Go on."

"I've had discussions with Paul Lumos from Episode Features. My attorneys have drafted up a merger agreement."

His father's face hardened, but he didn't seem surprised. "You went behind my back."

"You assigned me to run our publishing operations in New York. I'm doing what I feel is best. Frankly, I don't see any option. Together, Hunter Enterprises and EF can save on overheads that are threatening to kill us both. And I want to act now. Eighteen months down the track, it could be too late."

"You know, it's not the way I do business."

"Then, I'm sorry, but you need to change."

"I'm too old to change."

"Which is why you put me in charge."

Pushing to his feet, Guthrie crossed to the window, which overlooked the peaceful southern side of the property. As boys, Wynn and his brothers had pitched balls there, and roughhoused with Foxy, their terrier who had long since passed on. Wynn's mother had always brought out freshly made lemonade. She'd never gotten involved with the business side of things. Her talent had lain in cementing family values, keeping their nucleus safe and strong. When she'd passed away, the momentum of everything surrounding her had begun to warp—to keel off balance.

His father had remarried, then had needed heart surgery. The company had been split up among "the boys," and the siblings had gone off to live thousands of miles apart. Wynn's decision to mount this merger was just another turn in the road.

He waited for his father to argue more or, hopefully, see reason and acquiesce.

Guthrie turned to face him. "Now I have something I need to say."

Wynn sat down. "Go ahead."

"Christopher Riggs…"

Wynn waited. "What about Christopher?"

Guthrie pushed out a weary breath. "Vincent Riggs and I were having lunch a couple of months ago. His son joined us. Of course, I'd met Christopher before, but he's grown into such a focused man. Afterward, Vincent confirmed that Chris was extremely thorough—a dog with a bone when he got his teeth into a task. His background is investigative reporting."

When his father seemed to clam up, Wynn urged him on.

"I know Christopher's background." What was it that Guthrie wanted to say?

One of his father's hands clenched at his side. "I employed him," Guthrie said. "I gave him a job."

"You mean you had *me* give him a job."

"Son, I gave him the task of being my eyes and ears in New York."

Wynn sat back. He didn't like the feeling rippling up his spine.

"Why would you need him to do that?"

Before he'd finished asking, however, Wynn had guessed the answer. The righteous look on his father's face confirmed it. And then all the chips began to stack up. His insides curled into a tight, sick ball.

"Despite your objections to a merger, you suspected." Wynn ground out. "You knew I'd go ahead and put the deal together."

When Guthrie nodded, Wynn's pulse rate spiked before

he bowed forward, holding his spinning head in his hands. His throat convulsed. He had to swallow twice before he could speak.

"You hired that man to *spy* on me?"

"You mentioned mergers months ago. I needed to know what was going on." He moved closer. "Christopher admires you. It took a good deal to convince him."

"I'm sure a fat transfer into his checking account helped."

"I knew, out of all my boys, you would have the most trouble accepting why I would need to do something like this."

Understatement. Wynn felt it like a blunt ax landing on the back of his neck. "Who else have you got over in New York, sharpening their knives, waiting for the chance to stab me in the back?"

"This was a special circumstance. I needed to be able to step in. Defuse anything before promises were made I couldn't keep."

"Do Cole or Dex know?"

"No one knows."

Wynn swallowed against the bile rising at the back of his throat. His lip curled. "Guess we're even."

"We can move on from this."

"Until the next time you decide to go behind my back."

"Or you behind mine."

"I could go ahead without your approval," Wynn pointed out. He had the necessary authority.

His father slowly shook his head in warning. "You don't want to try that."

Wynn shot to his feet and headed for the door.

His father called after him. "You're more like me than you know."

"Yeah. We're both suckers." He slammed the door behind him.

He was striding down the hall when he ran into Dex.

"What the hell is wrong with you?" Dex asked, physically stopping Wynn as he tried to push around him.

"It's between me and the old man."

"Whatever it is, it couldn't be any worse than what we all went through yesterday."

"It's up there."

Wynn told Dex everything—about the merger plan, about the lowlife corporate spy, Christopher freaking Riggs. When Wynn had finished, his brother looked uncomfortable. Dex ran a hand through his hair.

"Geez, I wonder if he's ever sent anyone over to spy on me."

He'd needed his sons to take over the reins. None of them was perfect, but at least each brother was nothing but loyal to the family.

"He'd be better off sending someone to spy on his wife," Wynn growled under his breath. "If he thinks I betrayed him organizing a company merger, what the hell would he think of Eloise throwing herself at Cole, and God knows how many others?"

Dex gripped Wynn's arm and hissed, *"Shut up."*

"Why?" Wynn shook himself free. "You know the story better than me."

Dex was looking over his shoulder. Wynn paused and then an ice-cold sensation crept down his spine. He shut his eyes and spat out a curse at the same time his father's strained voice came from behind.

"Seems everyone knew the story but me."

With a sick feeling curdling inside, Wynn edged around. His father stood a few yards away. Leaning against the wall as if for support, his skin had a deathly pallor.

Wynn felt his own blood pressure drop. *What the hell have I done?*

From behind, he heard footfalls sounding on the pol-

ished wooden floor. As he stared at his father, he heard
Cole exclaim, "Eloise's water just broke. Dad, she's having the baby."

Twelve

Grace was headed downstairs when she heard a commotion. A woman was crying out as if she were in pain. Grace clutched the rail. What the hell was going on? Had that maniac stalker somehow struck again?

Below her in the vast foyer, Teagan appeared. Wynn's sister was helping Eloise to the front door. The older woman supported the weight of her big belly with both hands. Her stance was stooped and the grimace on the beautifully made-up face pointed to only one thing.

Grace fled down the stairs. She had not expected to be around for this. Wynn would want to stay longer now. It wasn't every day a person got to meet their new little brother or sister.

"Is there anything I can do?" Grace asked as she reached Teagan.

At that moment, Cole appeared. Rushing up, he let them know, "I just told Dad. He's on his way."

Eloise groaned, a guttural, involuntary, in-labor sound.

"Oh, *God*. We need to hurry." After another grimace, she started to pant.

"You'll be fine," Teagan told her. "Just try to relax. And nice deep breaths."

"I'll bring the car up," Cole said, flinging open one half of the double doors. "And where the hell is Dex?"

Suddenly Guthrie was there. The older man's expression was harried but not excited. His pallor, his shuffling gait…Wynn's father looked almost stricken. Wynn, who was coming up behind him, didn't look much better.

As Guthrie and Teagan escorted poor ambling Eloise out the door, Grace crossed over to Wynn. Worried, she cupped his bristled cheek.

"You look like you're ready to collapse."

He waited until everyone else was out the door, out of earshot, before he replied in a gravelly voice.

"I spoke with my father."

About the merger deal. "Guess he took the news badly."

Under her palm, a muscle in his jaw flexed twice. "He already knew."

Confused, she shook her head. "How?"

"And now he knows something else," Wynn muttered before wincing and rubbing his brow as if massaging the mother of all headaches. "I'm the world's biggest ass. I should have kept my freaking mouth shut," he groaned, clamping his eyes shut.

Grace tried to make sense of what he was saying but couldn't. "Wynn, Eloise is having the baby. You're going to be a brother again very soon."

He was shaking his head as if he wanted to block something out. Either they were staying or returning to New York. But if they were going to make that flight, they needed to think about getting to the airport.

"I opened my stupid mouth and now—" Resigned, he

exhaled and shrugged his broad shoulders. "Guess now I have to live with it."

Grace's heart was thumping high in her chest. "Wynn, please tell me what you're talking about."

His gaze—vacant and resigned now—met hers. He tried to tack up a tired smile. "There's no point dragging you into all this. You can't help. No one can."

As he grabbed her hand and they headed up the stairs, it took Grace all her willpower not to grill him again. But he was right. Whatever had happened between Wynn and his father, she couldn't help, no matter how much she might like to.

She and Wynn shared a certain spark. Aside from yesterday's near tragedy, these past days had been fun. But they were two individuals who had agreed to come together for a short time to enjoy a diversion. With bombs going off, things had gotten complicated enough. She shouldn't expect to get any more involved.

More to the point…Wynn clearly didn't want her involvement, either.

Later that evening, as Grace followed Wynn into Eloise's private hospital suite, she wished she were someplace else.

He'd decided they should stay and cancelled the flights. A couple of hours ago, when they'd received word that Eloise had given birth and both mother and child were doing well, Wynn had seemed less than enthusiastic.

Looking around the hospital suite now, the first thing Grace saw was a big white teddy bear with pink balloons and a sign that read, It's a Girl. Sitting up in bed, wearing a midnight blue nightgown set, Eloise looked radiant as she gazed down at her sleeping baby, who was wrapped in a pale pink blanket. Despite her complaints about being uncomfortable and "over it," she obviously adored this child.

While Shelby and Taryn were close enough to sigh over

the miniature fingers and that perfect baby face, Wynn's back remained glued to the wall. Dex looked uncomfortable, too. Guthrie stood on the opposite side of the room by a window, gazing upon the family scene from afar. No smile. Certainly he'd been through a lot these past hours, but Grace couldn't keep Wynn's earlier comment from her thoughts.

And now he knows something else.

Before coming to the hospital, she and Wynn, along with Dex and Shelby, had spent a quiet time with Tate. Wynn hadn't provided any more information about what had transpired between father and son that afternoon. She had vowed not to dig any more than she already had. But this situation, seeing Wynn so distant and cold, was cutting her to the quick.

Eloise was running a gentle fingertip around the baby's plump cheek. "Isn't she a honey? In fact, Honey would be a fine name." She glanced across at her husband. "Guthrie, darlin', you haven't had a hold. You know she looks just like you."

Wynn flinched. Muttering "Excuse me," he headed out the door.

Grace found him at the far end of the corridor. He seemed oblivious to the activity buzzing around him—nurses checking trays, mothers being wheeled to birthing suites. Gripping the wall behind his back, he looked haunted, as if he'd met a monster from his worst nightmare. She strode up to him.

Wynn wiped a palm down his face. Then, taking her arm, he led her into a small unoccupied waiting room.

Sitting together, he inhaled a fortifying breath.

"I didn't mean for him to hear," he began to explain. "I was blowing off steam. He must have followed me out of the study. I had no idea he was coming up behind me."

Blowing off steam. Grace's scalp began to tingle. "You mean your father? What did you say, Wynn?

"I said if anyone needed to be spied on, it was his wife." He angled toward her. "Can't you guess the reason Cole would rather avoid his beautiful, attention-seeking stepmother?"

When a thought crept in, too vile to contemplate, Grace shivered. She felt too stunned to breathe.

"Are you sure?"

"One holiday here in Australia, Eloise cornered Cole. Dex walked in and witnessed the tail end. Eloise had been trying to kiss Cole, caress him. She'd been drinking...." Wynn shuddered. "I never wanted to believe it. Now my father can't even look at me, or his wife, or his baby. After keeping it quiet all this time, Cole will be pissed when he finds out that Dad knows. He never wanted to be the bearer of that news. And Tate..."

Cringing, Wynn held his head in his hands. After a long tense moment, he sat back. His expression blistered with contempt.

"If I were Guthrie, I'd want to know. I'd want to know everything, straight up." He hung his head and then coughed out a humorless laugh. "You're probably thinking I wanted to give as good as I got."

That he'd meant to hurt his father through Eloise the same way he'd been hurt by Heather? God, no.

"I think there are times when lines get blurred."

"Between truth and deception? I'm not that naive." He found a grin. "Neither are you."

"I said that sometimes lines blur. Sometimes a person can unintentionally, well, *mislead*. Mislead themselves."

He thought about it and finally nodded. "Sure. I've convinced myself of things that turned out to be a lie."

"Me, too." She pulled down a breath. "The night Sam died," she said, "he proposed to me."

Wynn groaned and reached out to squeeze her hand with such tenderness, Grace could barely stand it.

"Wynn…" She swallowed. "I said no."

Wynn's expression stilled before doubt faded up to gleam in his eyes. "But…you *loved* Sam."

"I did love Sam." Her throat convulsed. "But more like a friend."

His brows swooped down. The grip on her hand tightened and then grew slack. "I'm confused."

"Sam and I dated for years. Everyone expected us to marry one day. I don't know if we started out in the same place and I grew in another direction, or if I was just too young to understand what I was getting myself into." Feeling heat burn her cheeks, she took a breath. "One minute we were kids, having fun. The next, people were asking when we were planning our big day."

Grace waited as the information sank in and Wynn slowly nodded.

"So, you turned Sam down," Wynn said, "he left, upset I imagine. And you never saw him again."

He paused and his eyes narrowed. "Did Sam say anything before he went?"

"Like what?"

"Like, I wish I was dead."

She recoiled. *Oh, God.* "Don't say that."

"But that's what's behind this confession, isn't it? What you've been thinking all these months after his accident. That you might have pushed him to it."

"I couldn't stop him from charging off," she explained, "getting in his truck. When I got word of the crash…"

The same raw regrets wound through her mind again. *If only I'd told him sooner. If only he hadn't taken the news so hard. If only I could have loved him the way that he'd loved me.*

"I never wanted to hurt Sam." She hesitated. "I'm not sure that Heather ever wanted to hurt you, either."

Wynn's face broke with a sardonic grin. "Hell, that's part of the attraction here, isn't it? Part of our bond. Only I didn't know it until now. Sam's tortured soul might be gone but I'm still here. You can't ask Sam just how bad it was, but you can ask me."

Before she could deny it, or admit he was right, Wynn went on.

"Well, I can tell you that the hours after Heather left me were the worst in my life. Jesus, I didn't *want* a life. My world was black, meaningless, and I couldn't see a way past it. So, if you're after some kind of absolution from me, I'm sorry, Grace. I just can't give it."

A tear spilled down her cheek. Wynn didn't have to forgive her. She hadn't expected that he would. The question was: would she ever forgive herself?

"I wish I could go back," she said. "Somehow make it right."

"There's no way back. All we can do is move forward. Call the truth the truth when we see it." He reached for her hand. "Avoid making the same mistakes."

Those words seemed to echo in her ears.

"That first night we met again," he went on after a moment, "we were clear on what we wanted. What we didn't want."

Grace remembered. She'd told him, *I'm not after a relationship...of any kind.*

"I'd always wanted a family of my own," he said. "When Tate came along, I decided I wanted a kid just like him." Taking a breath, he seemed to gather himself as he sat up straighter. "I don't want that anymore. None of it. I don't want to worry about infidelity or divorce or seeing my children every other weekend. I don't want permanent. No broken hearts. That's the God's honest truth."

A sound near the door drew their attention. A man walked in. His hair was rumpled like his shirt, but his smile was clear and wide; it spread more when he saw them sitting there.

"Hey, I have a boy!" he exclaimed as if he'd known them for years. "He's one hundred percent healthy." The man held his nose, as if he were trying to stem tears of joy. "He even looks like me. Same wing nut ears."

As the man headed for the coffee machine, Grace noticed someone else standing in the doorway. His head was hanging and a plastic dinosaur lay on its side near his sneakers. As she pushed to her feet, Wynn strode over and swung his little brother up on his hip.

"What are you doing here all by yourself, little man?"

"I ran down." Tate laid his head on Wynn's shoulder. "Teagan's coming."

A second later, Teagan appeared. She ruffled Tate's hair. "You're as fast as a cat, you know that?"

Putting on a brave face, Wynn hitched Tate higher. "Your baby sister's cute, huh?"

Tate rubbed a finger under his nose. "I guess."

Teagan dropped a kiss on Tate's cheek. "Doesn't mean we won't all love you just the same."

When Wynn pressed his lips to his brother's brow, a rush of emotion filled Grace's chest. Once he'd wanted a little boy just like Tate, but not anymore. At that wedding in New York, she'd told him that she wasn't after a relationship. She'd been clear. That had been *her* truth.

But now…

She didn't want to worry about infidelity or divorce, either. But one day she did want to get married. One day she wanted a child. A husband and family of her own. And she wanted to be closer to the family she had. She wanted to be near at hand to support Rochelle and April through the hard times ahead. Foremost, she wanted to truly get over the past, not just play at it. She thought she might finally be getting there.

No surprise. As much as that might hurt now, that meant a future without Wynn.

Thirteen

Two days after Eloise gave birth, Grace and Wynn landed back in New York. Wynn said she could stay at his place before she went back to Florida. She kept mum about her decision not to return there for good. Rather she said that she'd stay on with him an extra couple of nights.

He wanted to negotiate and they settled on five nights; after that explosion, they'd cut their stay in Australia short anyway. He'd have to make appearances at the office, he said. But Grace figured, with evenings all their own, five days would be enough for a proper goodbye.

When they arrived from the airport at Wynn's apartment, Grace headed for the attached bathroom where she ditched her travel clothes and slipped on a bathrobe. A few minutes later, she found Wynn, minus his shirt, standing in the middle of the master suite. He was studying his cell phone as if it might hold some answers.

"That was Cole," he said, looking up. "Apparently since we left, my father hasn't come out of his study."

Grace edged closer. Before leaving for the airport, Wynn had told his brother about his ill-timed slip regarding Eloise. "Does your stepmother know that Guthrie knows?"

"If she doesn't yet, my guess is she will soon." With a mirthless grin, Wynn rubbed his jaw. "My father's not the type to let a conflict go unresolved."

His young wife had sexually propositioned his oldest son—a humiliating kick in the gut. Guthrie would have suffered a complete loss of faith in Eloise—in his marriage. Still, some relationships could be repaired.

"Do you think they'll work it out?" she asked.

"Christ, I hope so. For the kids' sake."

That brand new baby, Honey, and, of course, Tate. When she and Wynn had left the Hunter mansion, his little brother had clung to Teagan's hand, a toy dinosaur clamped under his other arm. His chin had wobbled. He'd tried so hard not to cry.

"How's Tate?" she asked.

"Cole said he's missing us."

Missing Wynn. The Hunters didn't all get together often. Studies had proven that children benefited in so many ways from regular contact with extended family. That situation made her decision about being closer to her own family not only clearer but also vital. She'd made friends in Florida, in and outside of the practice. But when she'd left New York a year ago, Florida had merely been a means to escape.

She'd licked her wounds long enough. It was time to come home and, perhaps, start up her own practice. Years ago, when she'd decided on her college degree, that was the original plan. But she didn't want Wynn to think her decision to come home to stay, whenever he found out, had anything to do with *him.* It didn't. He'd told her—and in plain terms—he wasn't after "permanent." So, no need to further complicate this time together with info that didn't concern him. Wynn wouldn't want complications, either.

Now when he lifted her wrist and his mouth brushed the skin, a stream of longing tingled through her system. For these remaining days, she had every intention of acting on that physical desire. Then she would set those feelings aside. It made no sense to hang on to those emotions and fall in love with someone who would never love her back.

His arm wound around her at the same time his lips met hers. He kissed her until she was giddy and kneading his bare chest. By the time his lips left hers, her limbs were limp. This might not be forever but it was real and comforting and, for now, utterly right.

He swung her up into his arms and carried her over to the bed. When they lay naked on the sheet, he kissed her again—lazy and deep. Then his mouth made love to each of her breasts, her belly and then her thighs. She was coiling a leg around his hip, getting ready for his incredible icing on their cake, when he shifted and maneuvered her over onto one side.

The warm ruts of his abdomen met her back at the same time his tongue traveled in a mesmerizing line between her shoulder blades and up one side of her neck. As his palm sailed over her hip toward her navel, then her sex, her heightened physical need rushed to heat her blood. He explored her, delving and stroking until mad desire quivered and twisted inside of her.

Then he moved again, swinging her over. With her straddling him, he shifted her into position, aligned himself, and then thrust up, forcefully enough to send air hissing back through her teeth. Unsteady, she tipped forward, planting both palms on his pecs before his hands gripped her hips and she gave herself over to the heat and magic of his skill.

The strokes grew deeper, stronger, until each time he filled her, she pushed back and told herself never in her lifetime would she ever feel this good again. She'd never felt so connected, had never felt closer to anyone, to anything—

Her climax hit at the same time Wynn groaned and dragged her off him. Her fingers and toes were still curling when, out of breath, he gathered her close and buried his face in her hair. He ground out the words.

"I forgot."

Forgot what?

Then her eyes sprang open. She'd forgotten, too. They hadn't used protection. But he hadn't spilled inside of her.

"You pulled away in time," she said.

Which didn't mean a whole lot. Even with contraception, no one was a hundred percent safe. Every freshman knew a couple should never rely on withdrawal.

"We both got carried away," he said, urging her closer.

So true. But, no matter how carried away they'd both gotten, this was inexcusable.

"Wynn, that can never happen again."

He pressed a kiss to her brow. "You read my mind."

Which ought to have been the right response. No thinking person wanted an unplanned pregnancy, particularly between two people who had zero intention of spending their lifetimes together. And yet there was a part of her that felt—*disappointment?* Or, more simply, a sense of sadness.

One day she would find Mr. Right. Have a family. But she wasn't so sure about Wynn anymore. He was fun to be around. On so many levels he was caring, thoughtful. He was a good brother. An excellent lover.

But, deep at his core, Wynn could be cynical. Even bitter. He didn't believe in love—not for himself, in any case.

And it wasn't her place to convince him.

"In Greek mythology, Prometheus had returned the gift of fire to mankind. As far as Zeus was concerned, he'd overreached. The immortal was sentenced to an eternity of torment. A lifetime in hell."

Hunching into her winter coat, Grace listened in as a

local explained the story behind the famous Rockefeller Center statue to his tourist friend. Then he related how an engineer from Cleveland was contracted in the winter of 1936 to build a temporary ice-skating rink that had become a permanent fixture. Sometimes a bold idea panned out.

Sometimes it didn't.

Beside her, Wynn was on a call. Each time he spoke, vaporous clouds puffed out from his mouth. His black wool overcoat made his tall, muscular frame look even more enticing. When his gaze jumped across to her and he sent her a slanted smile, heat swam all the way through to her bones.

This afternoon, they'd strolled along Fifth Avenue, checking out the window displays at Saks, listening to carolers; Wynn's favorite Christmas song was "Winter Wonderland," and hers was "Silver Bells." No pressure. And yet, oftentimes Grace caught herself wondering where the two of them would be next holiday season—or five seasons from now.

Wynn finished the call and, with an apology, pulled her close.

"I'm taking you home, out of the cold," he said. "We can wrap presents." His lips grazed her cheek. "Do some *un*wrapping, too." His mouth grazed hers again. "I'll call Daphne and tell her I'm not coming back into the office."

"But you have a meeting about the merger this afternoon."

"That was Lumos. He postponed." He stole another feathery kiss. "I'm all yours."

Hand in hand, they headed down the Channel Gardens, a pedestrian street that linked to Fifth Avenue.

"Did you ever hear back from Christopher Riggs?" she asked, as the sound of carolers and the smell of roasting chestnuts wafted around them.

She'd been floored when Wynn had explained how

Guthrie had employed Riggs as a plant to feed back information regarding the possibility of a merger.

"Not a word," he said. "I figure, since he hasn't shown up at the office since I got back to town, my father must have gotten in touch and told him that his services were no longer needed."

"But you're going ahead with the merger. What if your father won't agree?"

"Then I'll have to reconsider my position here." He shoved his hands deeper into his coat pockets. "Times have changed. Are still changing, and fast. Business needs to keep ahead. I know a merger is the right way to go, and I can't twiddle my thumbs about it. I have to act now. If Hunter Publishing ever goes down, it won't be because I was a coward and didn't push forward."

So, he was willing to step down from his role at Hunter Publishing? She hoped this stalemate between father and son wouldn't come to that. And yet she saw in Wynn's expression now something that told her he wouldn't back down. Not because he was being stubborn but because he thought he was right. Typical Wynn.

But what was the alternative? He was convinced his company needed to evolve in order to survive and, hopefully, grow. If he couldn't make this deal happen—if a drastic change wasn't made—to his mind, he'd be knowingly committing corporate suicide.

She shunted those thoughts aside as he wrapped an arm around her waist.

"So," he leaned in toward her, "about that unwrapping…"

Her stomach swooped. He knew very well what day it was. Their agreement had been for her to stay at his place five nights. She'd made plans and, however much it cut her up inside, she needed to stick to them.

"I'm staying at Rochelle and April's tonight. We're putting a new star on their tree." Her heart squeezed for her sister and niece's situation. "Trey's not coming home for Christmas."

"Poor kid." His mouth tightened. "Another marriage bites the dust."

Grace understood the attitude, but his tone made her wince. He'd had his heart broken. Hell, Grace had broken someone's heart, too. But a man and a woman *could* build a happy life together. If they met at the right time, if they shared similar values, were prepared to commit—if they believed in their love, in their future, marriage could absolutely work out.

"So, you're staying at your sister's place tonight."

She nodded. "Flying to Florida tomorrow."

To formally resign and make arrangements to sublet her apartment there. In the New Year she would be back in New York and find a new door to hang her speech therapist sign on.

"But you'll be spending Christmas with your family, won't you?" he said as they turned onto Fifth Avenue.

"I thought I'd fly back up a couple of days beforehand." And stay—at her parents' home initially—until she found a place of her own.

"An invitation came through this morning," he said. "A Christmas Eve masquerade ball. All monies raised go to the Robin Hood Foundation."

Grace knew the charity. She supported their work helping all kinds of people in need. But she couldn't accept Wynn's invitation.

"You go." He would be generous with his donation either way. "I've already let my family know. I'm staying in with them Christmas Eve."

"You can change your mind."

"No, Wynn. I can't."

He didn't respond other than to tighten his grip on her hand.

When they passed a window display featuring a well-dressed snowman, she tried to edge the uneasiness aside. She wanted to enjoy what little time they had left together.

"Whenever I see a snowman," she said, "I think of that Christmas in Colorado."

When he didn't reply, she glanced across at him. Pre-occupied, he was looking dead ahead. Fitting a smile into her voice, she tried again.

"You were the snottiest boy I'd ever met. You were always so serious."

"I've been thinking," he said. "This doesn't have to end. You and me. Not completely. I could fly down to Florida. You'll be up here to see family. And we can always get away again. Maybe to the Bahamas next time."

Grace hung her head.

She'd anticipated this moment. Wynn didn't want to say goodbye. Not completely. But *she* didn't want to risk this affair going on any longer. Every day she felt herself drawn all the more. Breaking off now, for good, was hard. One of the most difficult things she'd ever had to do.

But how much more difficult would it be if they went on and on until she had to admit to herself, and to Wynn, she wanted more. It might not have started out that way but, ultimately, she would be after a commitment that he couldn't give.

He thought they could get away again sometime…

She tried to keep her tone light. "I don't think that'll work."

His frown was quickly interrupted by a persuasive smile. "Sure it can."

"No, Wynn." *I'm sorry.* "It can't."

When he stopped walking, she stopped, too. His gaze had narrowed on hers, as if he were contemplating the best way to convince her. To *win*. Finally, his chin kicked up and he took her other hand, too.

"Let's go home and we'll talk—"

"Your apartment isn't my home, Wynn, it's yours. I was only a guest." She hadn't even unpacked her bags properly.

"You can come and stay any time you like," he said.

"For how long? One month? One year? As long as it's not permanent, right?"

Her heart was thumping against her ribs. As she drew her hand from his, his brow creased even more.

"Where did all that come from?"

"We had an agreement. We extended it. Now it's over."

"Just like that?"

"Tell me the alternative."

He shrugged. "We go on seeing each other."

"When we can. Until it ends."

Her throat was aching. She didn't want to have this discussion. Wynn had been burned—now he was staying the hell away from those flames. His choice. But she had to do what was best for her. She had to protect her heart. She had to get on with her life.

Her phone rang. Needing a time out, Grace drew her cell from her bag and answered.

"I wanted you to know," Rochelle began, sounding concise but also breathy. "It was scary at the time, but everything's fine now."

Grace pushed a finger against her ear to block the noise of nearby traffic as Wynn, hands back in pockets, frowned off into the distance.

"What was scary?" she asked.

"April was admitted to the hospital this morning."

Grace's heart dropped. She pressed the phone harder to her ear.

"What for? What happened?"

"She was on a play date," Rochelle said. "Cindy's mother knew about the allergies. No nuts. Not a hint. Apparently

an older sister had a friend over who'd brought some cookies…"

Rochelle explained that when April had begun to wheeze
and complain of a stomachache, the mother had called
Rochelle right away. April's knapsack always carried an
epinephrine auto-injector in case of just this kind of emergency. Her niece had spent the next few hours in the E.R.
of a local hospital under observation. Sometimes there was
a second reaction hours later. Not this time, thank God.

"We're at Mom and Dad's now," Rochelle finished.

"I'll come straight over."

"You don't have to do that. I just wanted you to know."
Rochelle paused. "But if you can make it, I know April
would love to see you. Me, too."

When Grace disconnected, Wynn's expression had eased
into mild concern. He cupped her cheek.

"Everything okay?"

Grace passed on Rochelle's news. "I need to go and give
them both a big hug."

Wynn strode to the curb and hailed a cab in record time.
But when he opened the back passenger-side door, Grace
set a hand on his chest.

"You don't need to come," she said.

"Of course I'll come."

An avalanche of emotion swelled, poised to crash over
the edge. She shook her head. "Please. Don't."

As traffic streamed by one side of them and pedestrians
pushed past on the other, Wynn's gaze probed hers. For a
moment, she thought he was going to insist and then she
would have to find even more strength to stay firm when
all she really wanted to do was surrender and let him comfort her. But that was only delaying the inevitable.

His look eventually faded beneath a glint of understanding. She could almost feel awareness melt over him, and

see the consequences of "what comes next" pop into his head. In his heart, Wynn knew this was best.

"What about your bags?" he asked.

"I'll arrange to have them picked up."

"No. I'll send them on. I've got your father's address."

Leaning in through the passenger doorway, he spoke to the driver. "The lady's in a hurry," he said before stepping back.

On suddenly shaky legs, she slid into the cab. Before Wynn could close the door, she angled to peer up at him.

"I really did have the best time," she said.

His jaw flexed and nostrils flared before his shoulders came down and he nodded. "Me, too."

And then it was done. The door closed. The cab pulled away from the curb and she rode out of Wynn Hunter's life for good.

Fourteen

The next day, Wynn sat in his office, staring blankly at an email message his father had sent. He'd read it countless times.

Son, you have my blessing.

His eyes stinging, Wynn's focus shifted to the final merger document waiting on his desk. All the *i*'s were dotted. Every *t* crossed. Bean counters were happy and public-relations folks were beaming over the positive spin they could generate. In an hour, signatures would be down and the deal would be done.

Thank God.

He had his father's consent, but did he really have his approval? Did Guthrie understand that his son had acted only in the best interests of Hunter Publishing? Of the family? Which brought to mind that other predicament. The issue surrounding his father's marriage. The question of infidelity. Of trust. And desire.

He glared at his cell phone and finally broke. A moment later, he was waiting for Grace to pick up. When the phone continued to ring, he thought back and analyzed the situation.

There was no reason for her to be upset with him. After her niece's allergic reaction scare, Grace had been told that the little girl was home and fully recovered. Nevertheless, naturally he'd wanted to jump in that cab and keep her company—offer his support.

Yes, he'd wanted her to come to that charity ball Christmas Eve. If at all possible, he'd wanted her to stay a few more nights. Sure, the vacation was over but he wanted to see her again. Way more than he could have ever imagined. He cared for Grace a great deal.

Enough to continue to push the point?

He hadn't changed his mind about relationships, particularly after pondering the future of his father's second marriage. And it seemed Grace hadn't changed her mind about not wanting a serious relationship, either. Yesterday she'd been blunt. They'd had an arrangement. Now it was over. She didn't want the tie.

The line connected. Grace said hello.

"Hi." He cleared his throat. "Just making sure your niece is okay."

"April's fine. Thank God."

He closed his eyes. Just her voice… The withdrawal factor after only twenty-four hours was even worse than he'd thought.

"Did your bags get to your parents' address?"

"Yes. Thanks. I really appreciate it."

A few seconds of silence passed before he asked the question. "So, you're leaving for Florida today?"

"On my way to the airport now."

Wynn paused to indulge in a vision: him jumping in a cab and cutting her off at the pass. Crazy-ass stuff. Better to simply let her know his thoughts. His—*feelings*.

"Wynn, you there?"

"I'm here."

"I need to pay the driver. I'm at the airport."

"Oh. When's your flight?"

"Soon."

He heard a muffled voice—the driver, Wynn presumed.

"Sorry," she said. "I really have to go."

The line went dead. Wynn dropped the phone from his ear and rewound the brief conversation in his head. Then he stared at that merger contract again. He was about to sit back, rub his brow, when his cell phone chimed. Jerking forward, he snatched it up.

"Grace?"

A familiar voice came down the line. "Hey, buddy."

Wynn slumped. "Hey, Cole."

"Before I start, I want you to know that no one, including Dad, blames you for the fallout from your slip last week."

Cold comfort.

"Where is he with it?" Wynn grunted. "Filing for divorce?"

"*No.* He and Eloise have spoken. Are speaking."

Well, that was something.

"I'll keep you up to date," Cole said.

If only he could take it back. Of course, he didn't condone Eloise's behavior. He simply hadn't wanted to be the unwitting messenger, particularly when things in Sydney were crap enough for his father as it was.

"How's the investigation going?" Wynn asked.

"No one's easing up. Surveillance footage hasn't turned up any leads. Crime investigation is still tracking down possible links with the device's components. They're looking into DNA."

"And Brandon?"

"Everyone's in his sights, even his own men."

Off the job, Brandon Powell exuded a laid-back air, but beneath the cool sat a steely nerve. With his black belt in martial arts, a man would have to be nuts to pick a fight with that guy.

"Is there still a battery of security guards around the place?" Wynn asked.

"Twenty-four seven."

"And Tate?"

"When Tate begged to stay with his parents a bit longer, Dex and Shelby stayed on, too. Tate knows his parents are either avoiding each other or quarrelling. We all try to shelter him from it as much as we can, but Eloise isn't good with conflict."

Cole was being kind there.

Wynn was concerned about Tate coping with this situation, but none of this could be good for that baby—his half sister—either.

Wynn loosened his tie. Thank God he'd never have to go through anything like this. This whole situation sucked so bad, discussing it made him feel physically ill.

"I have something to ask," Cole said.

"Anything."

"Could you have Tate come for Christmas?"

Wynn blinked several times. "Where exactly is this coming from? How's Tate going to take that?"

"Tate's the one asking."

"And he asked to stay with me? Not Dex or Teagan or you?"

"He must want to spread the love. Or maybe he feels particularly safe with you. The way you rescued him that day—"

"He doesn't remember that."

"Maybe he does." Cole took a breath. "Can I put him on a flight next week?"

"Of course." *If that's what Tate really wants.* "Let me know the details when they're locked in." Dates, times, and obviously Tate would need a chaperone on the flight.

There were two beats of silence before Cole asked, "How's Grace?"

Wynn explained yesterday's conversation—how she wanted to end it and how he had complied.

Cole grunted. "How do you feel about that?"

"I feel…well, pretty crappy about it, actually."

"Because?"

He needed to ask? "Because we had a good time together."

"And?"

"And, I *like* her. But, Cole, she's right. We had an arrangement."

"What's that?"

Wynn hesitated a moment and then spilled it all—about Grace's ex, his proposal, the accident and how she wasn't interested in getting serious with anyone right now.

"What about you?" Cole asked.

"Of course, I was on board."

"Because of your bust-up with Heather."

Wynn ran his fingers through his hair. This wasn't rocket science. "Yes, because of my bust-up. I planned to marry the woman."

"Now you plan to stay single."

"Yes, sir, I do."

"And you told Grace that."

Wynn narrowed his eyes. "I told her. But you're missing the point. Cole, *she* was the one who wanted to end it."

"Smart girl."

Wynn cocked a brow. "I think I should feel insulted."

"Ask yourself something, and answer it truthfully. Are you falling in love with Grace Munroe?"

Wynn opened his mouth and then shut it again before he decided on a defense. "Just because you're happily married now—"

"Wynn, it doesn't have to be Grace, but I'd hate to see you lose someone meant for you because you're too damn stubborn and stuck to see what's right in front of your nose."

When they disconnected, Wynn was hot around the gills. Cole didn't understand. Wynn didn't need anyone second-guessing his life, his decisions, or telling him what he should or should not feel.

Five minutes on, Wynn had cooled down, not that it made him feel any better. His relationship with his father had been resurrected. The merger deal would go through. And yet, with all that he had…irrespective of all that "being right"…none of it seemed to matter alongside one simple, complicated truth.

He'd lost Grace.

Fifteen

A few days after Grace had flown down to Florida to re-sign her position, she was back in New York for the holi-days. Back in New York to stay, although she had yet to find a place of her own. Not that Wynn could know any of that.

When he sent a text to say his little brother was visit-ing for the holidays, naturally Grace was curious. Were Guthrie, Eloise and the baby here in the States, too? She doubted it. She'd responded, How cool! Tate would always have a very special place in her heart. Then a second text had mentioned that Tate loved to visit Rockefeller Center—every day at around two.

She knew she probably shouldn't. But she decided to go anyway.

Five minutes ago, she'd arrived at the Center and im-mediately spotted her boys. Dressed for chilly weather, the Hunter brothers were checking out skaters, laughing when-ever Santa slid around with a conga line of kids hanging off the back of his red suit. The giant tree towered over the crowd, rewarding everyone with glowing, festive thoughts. Like streams of sparkling atoms filling the air, on Christmas Eve, magic seemed to be everywhere.

As if he sensed her nearby, Wynn pulled up tall and scanned the crowd. When their gazes connected, a spark zapped all the way up her spine. His expression shut down before a smile tugged the corners of his beautiful mouth.

He didn't call her over. Rather he simply waited, drinking her in as if he worried that, should he look away, she might disappear. Then Tate tugged his brother's windbreaker and his little red beanie tipped back. Wynn crouched down.

Tate seemed to know that his big brother was distracted. When he spotted her, Tate jumped into the air, so high she thought his feet must have grown springs. Wynn placed a hand on his shoulder, but Tate refused to calm down. Grace heard his squeals for her to join them.

He was such a good kid, going through such a hard time. His family might have wealth but, no doubt, he would trade everything, and in a heartbeat, for a safe and settled home.

As she came closer, Tate broke away. In a bright blue parka and boots, he scampered up and flung his arms around her hips.

"This is a really big city," Tate said, still hugging her tight. "You found us anyway." He pulled back and looked up with the familiar tawny-colored eyes that stole her heart away. "The Empire State Building has a hundred and two stories."

She laughed. "Pretty high, huh?"

"Didja see the snowman in that window?" He pointed toward the avenue before he flapped his arms against his thighs and shrugged. "Santa's coming tonight. We need to finish the tree."

Wynn had strolled up. "And we need to get to bed before those reindeer swing their bells on into New York."

Grace's stomach fluttered at the sound of his voice—the

white flash of his smile. She had to dig her hands deeper into her pockets to stop them from reaching out.

"Mommy takes my picture when I put cookies out for Santa, but Wynn's gonna do it this year."

When Tate took his brother's leather-gloved hand, the picture, its setting, just seemed to fit.

Grace schooled her features. She was getting misty, damn it.

"Not going to that masquerade ball?" she asked Wynn.

"They have my donation." He winked at his little brother. "Tate and I have important things to do."

Tate gave a big nod. "Can Grace come over?"

Wynn arched a brow. "I think she already has plans."

"I'm staying with my parents," she told Tate. "My sisters will be there tonight. My niece, too. April's almost your age."

Tate's mouth hooked to one side, not in a happy way. "A girl?"

"Like Honey," Wynn said, "only older." Then he checked out the sky, which was heavy with the promise of snow. "We were getting ready to go for a hot chocolate—"

"Oh, sure," she slipped in. "I won't hold you up."

"I like mine with marshmallows on top," Tate said. "Wynn likes chocolate curls."

Grace jerked a thumb toward the street. "I really have to go. But I have something for you, Tate." She drew a wrapped gift from beneath her coat. Accepting it, Tate looked to Wynn. "He can open it now," she said.

Tate peeled the wrapping and eased out the gift. His legs seemed to buckle before he whooped with delight.

"A Yankees triceratops! His horn goes right through the cap!" Tate gave her an earnest look. "Santa can't beat this."

Grace held her throat. Her heart felt so full and at the same time so empty. She wished she could stay longer. But a fast, clean break would be best.

"After the holidays, Wynn's gonna take me to his office." Tate tugged his brother's coat. "Can I go see the skaters?"

"Sure, pal." When Tate was out of earshot, Wynn stepped closer. His gaze swept over her face, lingered on her lips.

"You look great," he said.

"You look—relaxed. Did your father come out with Tate?"

"Cole chaperoned him over on the flight. Tate had asked if he could come out."

Wynn didn't need to explain more. Grace thought she understood.

"Dad let me know he was okay with the merger going through," he went on.

"*Wow.* That's great. Congratulations."

"He and Eloise are trying to work things out."

She eased out a grateful breath. "I'll pray that they do."

He looked back at Tate standing a short distance away, checking out Santa, who was performing one very fine axel jump.

"It's good having Tate over," he said, "even if the circumstances aren't the best."

"Any progress on who was behind that explosion?"

"Not yet. But I'm sure they'll find something soon." He adjusted one leather glove then the other. "Dex and Shelby are flying over tomorrow afternoon. They're staying with her father in Oklahoma tonight. In fact, Mr. Scott is flying out here with them."

"A real family affair."

"He and Tate got to be chums when Dex took him out there for a stay."

"What are Cole and Taryn doing tomorrow?"

"Visiting Dad and the new baby. And Eloise, I suppose."

Awkward. "And Teagan? Is she flying out to be with Tate, too?"

"She says she isn't. When I spoke to her, I got the feeling it might have something to do with a man."

The man who wanted a big family? "Did she sound okay?"

"She sounded preoccupied."

As soon as she left here, Grace decided, she'd phone Teagan. She hoped her friend hadn't broken up with the guy she'd been seeing. If he was in love with her, and Teagan felt the same way, there had to be a way to sort everything out.

"I was wondering," Wynn said, crossing his arms, "whether you might like to come over tomorrow, too. I know you'd have all the traditional stuff in the morning with your family. And lunch. But if you're free for dinner, Tate would love to have you over. Dex and Shelby, too."

As he made the invitation, the ache in Grace's throat grew and grew. But she'd been prepared for something like this. Wynn didn't give in easily. Neither did she.

Over these past few days, with being away from Wynn and missing him so much, she'd come to a solid conclusion. She loved this man. Loved most everything about him. But she wasn't about to do anything foolish like admit it and set herself up for a gigantic fall. She'd seen firsthand how a move like that could destroy a person.

"Thanks for the invite," she said, proud of herself for holding his gaze. "But I can't. I'm sorry."

"No. It's fine. *I'm* sorry. Just had to ask. You know. For Tate."

Tate was gazing up at the big tree in wonder, holding his new dinosaur under his arm. So cute and innocent.

She swallowed.

God, her throat was tight. Clogged.

She really had to go.

"I'll just say goodbye," she said.

Wynn tried to smile. "You've only been here a minute."

She began to skirt her way around him.

"Stay a little longer," he said.

"I have to go."

"Grace." He caught her arm and her eyes finally locked with his. A soft smile touched the corners of his mouth. "Grace. I don't want to lose you."

She held her stomach. How blunt did she need to be? "Wynn, you don't want what I want."

"I want you."

"And I want *love*."

Her heart was thumping in her ears. She felt weak and emotional and, hell, it was *true*. And now, in a single heart-beat, it was out.

She watched understanding sink in and then resistance darken his eyes. Meanwhile, Tate had run back and was tugging on his big brother's coat again.

"Wynn, where's the hot chocolate shop? I'm cold."

Grace crouched down. She prayed Tate didn't see that she was trembling or that tears edged her eyes.

"You'll have a great Christmas with everyone, won't you, hon?"

"Are you gonna come, too?" Tate asked.

"Afraid not," she said.

Tate studied the Yankees dinosaur she'd given him. "Well," he said, "maybe next time."

When she looked up at Wynn, he was taking Tate's hand.

"Come on, buddy," he said. "Don't want that hot choco-late going cold."

They started off and then Wynn stopped, turned back around.

"Have a good day tomorrow, Grace," he said.

Forcing a smile, she nodded but couldn't say the words.

Merry Christmas.

Happy New Year.

It was past eight that night when Grace edged inside the room her niece used whenever she stayed at Grandma and

Grandpa's. The night-light was on, casting stars around the ceiling and walls.

"Is she asleep?" she whispered.

With a children's Christmas book closed on her lap, Rochelle had been gazing at her daughter.

"I thought I'd need to read *'Twas the Night Before Christmas* at least twice through." Rochelle eased to her feet. "April was counting sugar plums after the third verse." Crossing over, Rochelle saw the notebook Grace held. "You're working on exercises tonight?"

"Not the kind you think."

The women tiptoed out of the room. Downstairs, their mother was finalizing tomorrow's menu with Jenn. Dad would be reading in his chair. Tilly was out with friends, due home soon, or at least not late.

Grace led Rochelle into her room. The fire she'd lit earlier was crackling with low yellow flames while snow piled up on the windowpane outside. A gift she'd bought April that afternoon lay on the bed. When she and Rochelle sat on the quilt, Grace rapped her knuckles against the notebook's cover.

"I had something I needed to work through," Grace explained. "I thought writing it all down might help. It's about Sam." She bowed her head. "A year after the funeral, I still felt responsible."

"Because you didn't love him?"

"The night Sam died, he asked me to marry him." Everyone knew that he had planned to sometime very soon. "Rochelle, I said no. I turned him away."

Rochelle froze. "Okay, wait. You think he took his own life, or maybe he was so upset that he lost control of the vehicle?"

"Not anymore." Wincing, Grace gripped the book. "I mean, I don't know."

"He'd just gotten off a long shift. It was deemed an accident."

Grace finished for her. "Authorities surmised he'd fallen asleep at the wheel. But I couldn't put it to rest."

"So you kept it bottled up inside of you all this time?" Rochelle's hand covered hers. "Grace, you're not responsible for what happened to Sam. Just like I'm not responsible for Trey's actions."

"Yeah. I know, but…"

"Sam was taken away from us too soon. We were all lucky to have known him. But you can't change the past, and you can't change how you feel. If Sam were here now, he'd want you to let it go and really get on with your life."

Grace expelled a breath. Of course, Rochelle was right. Tonight, missing Wynn and wondering about the future, Grace had only needed to hear it, and from someone she trusted, despite any past sisterly spats.

That story finished, Grace slid the notebook into her bedside drawer and then eyed the velvet box containing April's gift. "What time's Trey collecting April tomorrow?"

"He isn't. Says it'll be too awkward for her." Rochelle rolled her eyes. "Makes me all the more determined. This Christmas is going to be extra special—with plenty of family and love to go around. Every kid deserves that."

Grace picked up April's gift and flipped open the lid. A huge crystal ring shone out. "Think she'll like it?"

"April?" Rochelle gave a low whistle. "Heck, I want it myself."

Grace cut the paper while Rochelle ripped off some tape.

"Have you heard from Wynn?" Rochelle asked, pressing a glossy pink bow on top.

Grace had confided in Rochelle about that afternoon when she'd called after April's allergy scare. She spilled all about her tormented feelings toward Wynn as well as her decision to stay clear. To protect her heart.

"I saw him today." Grace set aside the wrapped gift. "His little brother's out for the holidays."

"I thought you said you two were through."

"We are. But Tate asked to see me. After all that kid's been through, I wasn't going to stand him up."

"Oh, Grace, are you sure you want to end it? You had such a great time in Australia."

"Aside from the explosion."

"Aside from that." Rochelle leaned forward. "The way you feel about each other...the things he says and does..."

"Are all *incredible*. Addictive is the word. But Wynn isn't interested in strings." She fell back on the bed and stared at the ceiling. "He doesn't want the hassle."

"He might change his mind."

No. "I need to get on with my life."

Grace's cheeks were hot, her throat thick. She sucked down a breath and, determined, pulled herself up. She was moving on.

"For now," she said, calm again, "that means helping you bring Santa's presents in from the garage." Swiping April's gift from the quilt, she headed for the door. "One extra-special Christmas coming up."

Wynn jingled the ornament at the overdecorated tree, which was set up in a prime corner of his apartment's living room.

"This is the very last bell."

Tate pointed to a spot on a lower branch. "Here."

After securing the bell in place, Wynn pushed to his feet, flicked a switch and the tree's colored lights blinked on, flashing red and green and blue.

Tate squealed. "We did it!"

"Of course we did! We can do *anything*."

They jumped into a "dice roll" move and finished with a noisy high five.

"Now, we need to put out those cookies for Santa," Wynn said, shepherding Tate toward the open-plan kitchen.

"And take a picture to send to Mommy."

Tate dropped some red tinsel on the special Santa plate while Wynn broke open a new batch of cookies. When the milk was poured, they moved to the dining table and set the snack up. They took a photo and sent it through to Australia. Within seconds, they got a reply.

Looks delicious! Love you, baby.

Tate read the message ten times over. When he said, "Send it to Grace," Wynn hesitated. He'd sent her a couple of messages during the week and when she'd shown up that afternoon at the rink, frankly, he'd almost begged her to stay. And then things had gone a little far afield. At first he hadn't been sure what she'd said. He'd only known the word *love* was involved.

She'd put it out there. What she'd wanted had changed. Or shifted one hell of a lot forward. At Cole's wedding, before that explosion, he might have been swayed. Knowing he was at least in part responsible for the possibility of his father's marriage ending—knowing the added crap this small boy would need to endure if that union ultimately broke down for good... Why the hell would he, would anyone, knowingly risk that much? When things went south, it just freaking *hurt* too much.

His jaw clenched tight and he lowered the phone. "How about we send the snap to Grace in the morning?"

Hopefully, with everything else happening and their visitors arriving, Tate would forget about it.

"Won't Grace like the picture?"

"Well, sure. She'd love it. It's just getting late. She's probably already in bed."

"She could still find it in the morning when she wakes up."

"Which is why we ought to send it then."

"We might forget."

"No way."

Tate blinked. "Please, Wynn."

Wynn took in his brother's uncertain expression, the mistrust building in his eyes. "You're right," he said, thumbing a few keys. "There. Sent."

They waited. No reply came through. But Wynn simply explained, "See. Told you she'd be asleep by now. We should be, too."

Picking up Tate, he swirled him through the air until his brother was giggling madly. Then they moved to the guest bathroom, where Tate brushed his teeth. After Wynn had bundled his brother into bed, he saw the distant look in Tate's eyes. Was he thinking of his home?

"Do you miss your Mom, Tate?"

He fluffed the covers. "Daddy, too. But I'm kinda used to it."

"Being away?"

Tate nodded. "I had lots of fun with Dex and Shelby. With Teagan and Damon, too."

"Damon's Tea's friend, right?"

"He likes Tea a lot. Like you and Grace. They hold hands and laugh."

Wynn cleared the thickness from his throat. "Sounds good."

Tate's head slanted sideways on the pillow. "Why didn't Grace want to come home with us?"

"It's Christmas Eve. Grace is with her family."

Tate flashed a gappy grin. "I'm glad I'm here with you."

"Things must seem a little...mixed up back home."

"That's not why I wanted to come. I thought you'd be lonely. I thought we could hang."

Wynn smiled but then sobered. "Why did you think I'd be lonely?"

Tate frowned but didn't say anything.

"Things aren't as good as they could be back home," Wynn said. "But you need to remember that everyone loves you very much—your parents, your brothers, Tea. Me. Family's very important."

"If that's right, Wynn, why don't you want a little boy of your own?"

Wynn stopped breathing. "Why would you say that?"

"You said so. You don't want to have a son like me, or family, or anything."

"Did you hear that at the hospital?"

"Tea wanted something hot to drink. I ran ahead. You and Grace were there, talking." He fluffed the covers again. "It's okay. I don't want to be a dad, either. Kids only get in the way. Mommies only ever sleep or cry." His voice lowered. "Mommy says it's all your fault. Don't know why."

Wynn did. If he'd kept his big mouth shut, Guthrie wouldn't have overheard his bleating to Dex about Eloise coming on to Cole.

Tate pushed out a sigh. "I'm pretty sure it's my fault though. That's the other reason we should have Christmas together. No one else has to feel mad or sad when we're around."

It felt as if a giant hand was squeezing the life from his windpipe. Tate thought it was *his* fault?

Wynn's voice cracked as he said, "I'm so sorry about what's happening at home." He'd never been more sorry about anything in his life.

"Aw, Wynn. Don't cry." Tate reached to cup his big brother's face. "You're perfect."

A serrated knife twisted high in Wynn's gut. He ran a hand over his little brother's head. So soft and sweet and unreservedly worthwhile. His own childhood had been great. He'd known he was loved and adored by both parents. That's why he'd been so sure about having a family of his own. Then Heather had done him in and all of that no longer mattered. Except…

Now, looking deeper, that *hadn't* changed. In this moment, that dream seemed like the only thing that *did* matter. What the hell was the point of being here if he couldn't be with the person that he—?

That he what exactly? Just how deeply did he feel about Grace?

"I want you to know that if ever I had a boy of my own," he croaked out, "I'd want him to be just like you."

"That's not what you said. You said if you never had a family of your own, you wouldn't miss it."

"You're wrong." Drawing back, Wynn shook his head. "No. *I* was wrong. I was sad and confused. I haven't, well, been myself lately. But I do want a son."

Tate touched his big brother's cheek. "I think Grace is mad at you, too."

"I don't blame her." Wynn found Tate's hand on his cheek and set his jaw to stem the emotion. "We're just going to have to fix it, is all."

"Do you think that we can?"

"Of course we can. Remember?" Wynn smiled. "You and I can do anything."

Sixteen

Early the next morning, with all the presents opened, April was twirling around the Munroe's twelve-foot tree showing off the new pink princess costume that Santa had brought. There were coloring books and puzzles and a bike with training wheels, too. Grace liked to think her niece's favorite gift was the big crystal ring she'd received from her aunt. When she'd opened the box, April's eyes had bugged out. The ring hadn't left her finger since.

Now Grace sat on a couch sampling a perfume that Tilly had hoped she would like—sweet and sassy, just like her younger sister. Her father stood by the window that overlooked the vast backyard and, beyond that, a park. Children had constructed a snowman there—hardly anything new for this time of year. Still, this morning the sight created a giant lump in Grace's throat.

Wynn and that long-ago Christmas were in her thoughts constantly. After seeing him with Tate yesterday, she'd barely been able to sleep. She imagined she heard his laugh.

She closed her eyes and saw his sexy, slanted smile. She felt so filled with memories, she wondered if her family could see them mirrored in her eyes. Smell them on her skin.

April twirled over and presented a large gold and crimson Christmas bonbon.

"I'll let you win," April said.

Grace grabbed an end and angled her wrist just so, but when April tugged hard, the gold paper ripped and she won the prize—a green party hat and tiny baby doll.

Rochelle was checking out the foot spa Grace had given her. "My toes can't wait to use this," she said, wiggling her slippered feet.

"And I can't wait to wear these." Her mom was showing off a silk scarf and sapphire drop earrings.

Grace forged her way through a sea of crumpled paper to join her dad. He had three new ties slung around his neck.

"More snow's on the way," he said, surveying the low, gray sky.

April's voice came from behind. "Didn't stop Santa last night. Mommy, can I ride my bike?"

Rochelle was studying the titles on a CD, a gift from Tillie who, earphones in, was tapping her foot to a tune belting out of her new iPod.

"It might be too slippery." Rochelle pushed up and crossed over to the duo parked by the window. Then she poked her nose closer to the pane. "That's a mighty fine looking snowman."

April squealed. "Can I go see?"

Grace turned around and tapped April's tiara. "I'll take you. I want to see him, too." She crouched before her niece. "But our guy looks as if he's missing a hat and pipe."

"That's my job." Grandpa headed off. "I put them away in the same place every year."

She and April pulled on their boots, shrugged into coats and worked their fingers into mittens or gloves. April took the hat from Grandpa, Grace the pipe, and together they headed out down a shoveled path rimmed with glistening snow. As they passed through the side gate, April scooted on ahead.

"Be careful!" Grace called out. "Don't slip. You don't want to get your princess skirt wet."

When Grace caught up, April was skipping about the snowman.

"He's so tall!" Her niece held out the hat. "I'll put it on."

Grace lifted April high and she very carefully positioned the battered fedora on the snowman's head. When Grace put April down, the little girl stood back. With her mittened hands clasped under her chin, she inspected her work.

"It's crooked."

"I think it lends him character."

"What's that?"

"It means snowmen are more fun when their hats don't sit straight."

But if Wynn were here, Grace thought, he would want to straighten it, too.

"You can do the pipe." Examining the snowman, April tilted her head and her beanie's pink pom-poms swung around her neck. "Put it in crooked."

Grace slid the pipe in on one side of the snowman's mouth, and then flicked it up a tad.

April danced around the snowman again, her pink princess skirt floating out above her leggings while she sang. Then she stopped and trudged closer to their man.

"Something's up there." April pointed. "On his broom." She gasped. "Presents!"

Grace trod around and looked. Sure enough, two wrapped gifts were dangling from the rear of the snowman's broom. She leaned in closer. Were they tied to shoelaces?

"Whatever they are, we should leave them be." Grace

took April's hand as she reached for the gifts. "They don't belong to us."

"They do, too. Santa left them." April glanced around. "Maybe he left more."

"They're for decoration."

April wouldn't listen. Only her eyes appeared to be working—they were wide, amazed. Grace sighed. If April was disappointed when those boxes ended up being empty, perhaps Aunt Gracie could leave something special out here later to compensate.

Grace untied the gifts and handed them over. April would accept only one.

"That one's for you," April said.

Grace peeled off her wrapping while she kept an eye on April. They both got to their boxes at the same time and flipped open the lids. April let out a sigh filled with wonder.

"It a Christmas watch!"

When April tried to slide the white leather band off its looped holder, Grace helped. April slipped the oversize watch over one mitten, and then held her arm out to admire it.

"It has a Christmas tree," April murmured.

"And Christmas balls at the ends of the hands."

"What about yours?"

Wondering now if they ought not to have opened the boxes—clearly these were meant for someone else, perhaps the neighbors—Grace examined her watch face. "Mine has a snowman—" she blinked, looked harder "—with a crooked hat."

"Why did Santa leave them out here?"

Grace was about to admit she had no idea when a voice replied for her.

"He wanted to let us know that it's time to count our blessings—past, present and, hopefully, future."

On suddenly wobbly legs, Grace turned around while April crept forward.

"Gracie, someone's standing behind our snowman."

Wynn stepped into view. He wore a black sweater and windbreaker and pale blue jeans. With his dark hair ruffling in the breeze, he'd never looked so handsome.

When April whispered *"Who is he?"* Grace was brought back to the moment and replied, "I think he must be lost."

Wynn stepped forward and his one-in-a-million energy radiated out. The wind was cool and yet she might have been standing on a hot plate.

"I don't feel lost. Not anymore." He glanced at the sky. "Snow's coming—any minute, I reckon."

Smooth. He was after an invitation. "I'd invite you in, but—"

"I brought someone with me," he cut in, and nodded toward a vehicle Grace hadn't noticed until now. Tate was waiting by the hood. All bundled up for the weather, he arced an arm over his head, waving.

April tugged her aunt's jacket. "Do you know him? Is he nice? Can I say hi?"

Wynn answered April. "I'm sure he'd like that."

Still, April looked to her aunt with pleading eyes. Giving in, Grace straightened April's beanie.

"Sure. Go ahead."

Her tiny boots crunching in the snow, April trundled away. When she stopped before Tate, April hesitated before extending her hand to give him a look at what Santa had left.

Grace had put it together. "You built this snowman."

"Me and Tate."

"How did you know I'd come out to have a look?"

"I'd like to think I know you pretty well."

When he edged closer and reached out, Grace was ready to push him away—no matter how much she might want to, she wouldn't change her mind about rebooting their affair. But he only gestured at the watch.

"You like it?" he asked. "They're matching *his* and *hers*."

As in *you* and *me?* "You're not going to get that watch back from April."

His crooked grin said, of course not. "Tate brought a gift especially for your niece."

Near the vehicle, Tate was holding the watch, inspecting the face, while April ogled a necklace decorated with huge sparkling blue and clear "jewels." The two kids began to talk, and then laugh.

"That's a good sound," Wynn said. "Reminds me of when we were kids."

"I don't remember you laughing very often."

"Perhaps because I expected too much."

She crossed her arms over her coat. "I don't expect too much." She only knew what she needed. What she'd accept.

She didn't want to sound harsh but neither would she back down. What they had shared had been a wonderful but also brief journey. He wanted the fun times to go on. She'd made herself a promise. She needed to get on with her life. And Wynn didn't want to be a part of that. Not in the long term.

Wynn was studying the snowman. "Tate and I had a talk last night. It opened my eyes to a lot of things. Honesty can slog you between the eyes," Wynn said. "But we get back up. A couple of months ago, my truth was that I needed some release. Some fun. A connection. I found that with you. And I found a lot more."

Nearby, snow crunched as if someone had fallen, and then a little cry ripped out. A few feet away, Tate lay face down. Without missing a beat, April shot out her hand. Tate wrenched himself up and then they set off, running around again.

"I wonder if they'll remember this day," she said, watching as the kids stopped to pat together two snowballs.

"My bet is, as clearly as I remember that day in Colorado when I tripped over my lace."

She narrowed her eyes at him. "After all these years, now you remember it that way?"

"I remember that I'd agonized over whether or not to give you a gift."

"A poke in the eye?"

"A bunch of flowers, plastic, lifted from a vase in one of the chalet's back rooms. But then I thought you might want to hug me or something gross like that, and it seemed easier to pretend I didn't like you."

Her smile faded. "We're not kids playing games anymore."

"No. We're not."

He leaned forward just as a snowball smashed against his shoulder. Tate stood a short distance away; given his expression, he didn't know whether to run or laugh or fastball another one. Beside him, April's pom-poms were dancing around her neck, she was giggling that hard. She pitched her baby snowball and bolted in the other direction. Tate followed.

Grinning, Wynn swiped snow off his jacket. "Naughty and nice."

"Is Tate missing his folks?"

"He knows they're arguing. He's not sure why. He thinks it's his fault. Well, his and mine. That's why he wanted to come over from Sydney. So we pariahs could hang together."

Her heart clutched and twisted. "That's so sad."

"We'll work through it, me and Tate—and the rest of the family. Sometime in the New Year, I'm going back to... well, face it all."

Grace cast a glance toward the house. Her father was

peering out the window again. She thought of all the food and warmth and company inside that house. She could hear Tate and April playing some game together and, after listening to what poor Tate was going through, it seemed wrong not to ask.

"Wynn, would you and Tate like to have breakfast with us?"

His somber expression faded into a soft smile. "We'd like that very much. There's something else I'd like even more." His eyes searched hers. *"You."*

She shivered with longing, with need, but she wanted more than "just for now," and she refused to feel guilty because of it.

"Wynn, we don't need to go through this again."

"We really do."

The knot high in her stomach wrenched tighter. He was making this so hard. "I want a family of my own, Wynn. Don't you get it?"

"Me, too. So, we need to get married. The sooner the better."

She'd come to terms with him showing up unannounced, organizing the snowman, the gifts. But this? A proposal? She wanted to be hopeful, excited. But a man didn't change his mind about something like that overnight.

"I didn't believe it," he went on, "that it could happen that fast. Falling in love, I mean."

Her back went up. "I can't help how I feel."

"Not you. *Me.*" His gloved hand slid around the back of her waist. "I love you," he said, and then broke out into a big smile. "Damn, that felt good."

Time seemed to stop. She set her palm against his chest to steady herself as her head began to spin.

"This isn't happening," she said.

"Close your eyes and I'll prove that it is."

When his mouth slanted over hers, her eyes automatically drifted shut and, in an instant, she was filled up with his warmth—with his strength. And then the kiss deepened and a million tiny stars showered down through her system—her head and her belly. Most of all, her heart. When he drew her closer, she stood on the toes of her boots and curled her arms around the padded collar at his neck. He tilted his head at a greater angle and urged her closer with a palm on her back until they were pressed together like two pages in a book.

When his lips finally left hers, she couldn't shake herself from the daze. His face was close and had a contented expression. In his eyes she saw every shade of "I'm certain." And the way he was holding her... No matter what she said, he wasn't about to let her go.

"I love you, Grace. The kind of love that can't take no for an answer. The kind that just has to win out."

While deepest emotion prickled behind her eyes, snow began to fall, dusting their hair and their shoulders. A snowflake landed on the tip of his nose at the same time a hot tear rolled down her cheek.

"Marry me," he said in a low, steady voice. "Be my wife. My love forever."

She swallowed deeply. Tried to speak.

"This isn't a rebound, is it?" she asked.

He only grinned. "Not a chance. I want you to have my name. Grace Hunter. Mrs. Wynn Hunter. I want to have babies with you and work through all those ups and downs families face. The challenges and triumphs that will make us even stronger."

Two little voices drifted over.

"He's gonna kiss her again."

"Gracie's gonna be a princess bride."

When she and Wynn both looked over, the kids darted away. Wynn's voice rumbled near her ear. "Smart kids."

He kissed her again, working it until she was mindless,

boneless—completely, unreservedly his. When his mouth gradually left her, she had to grip his windbreaker while her brain tried again to catch up.

"Can you see the future?" he asked. "Me in a tuxedo, Dex and Cole standing at my side. Your father is walking you down the aisle and our guests are sighing, you look so beautiful. So happy."

A breath caught in her throat. And then she realized. He was right. She could see it, too. Their families were there—all of them.

"Tate will be a ring bearer," she murmured, as another drop slid down her cheek, "and April the flower girl."

"And?"

"And…" She cupped his jaw then ran fingers over that faint scar on his temple. He was waiting for her answer. It seemed the *only* choice.

"I love you," she said. "I can't wait to marry you."

The snow was falling harder, catching on his lashes, in the stubble on his jaw, and as he kissed her again, everything in their world—everything in her heart—felt incredible. Amazing. Just the way it ought to.

"Would you believe," he said as his lips slipped from hers, "I don't have a ring."

A little hand tugged Grace's coat. One of April's mittens was off and she was offering up her crystal solitaire.

Grace laughed she was so touched, and Wynn cocked his head. "Wow. April, are you sure? That looks like a lot of carats."

Tate held April's hand. "I'll get her another one."

A call came from the house—it was Grace's father telling everyone to come in. When Tate looked up at his brother, Wynn said, "Go ahead, buddy."

As they watched the young couple trot toward the path, Grace linked her arms around her fiancé's neck.

"Guess we ought to go in, too," she said. "Snow's coming down pretty fast."

"Let it snow," he said. "I *love* the snow. I love you." Cupping her cheek, he smiled adoringly into her eyes. "Today all my Christmases have come at once."

Epilogue

Meanwhile in Seattle...

Crouched on her bathroom floor, Teagan Hunter hugged herself tight, and then groaning, doubled over more. Her stomach was filled with barbed wire knots, but the pain went way beyond physical. It was memories. It was regrets. They circled her thoughts like a pack of vultures waiting to drop.

The High Tea Gym had barely seen her all week, and that had to change. She had a business to run, bills to pay, staff to supervise and clients to inspire. But then those vultures swooped again and Teagan only had the strength to lower her brow to her knee.

Her determined side said this was a case of mind over matter. She'd be fine. She would endure. No. She would *flourish*. God knew, up until now, she'd coped with a lot in her life. Still, she couldn't shake another voice gnawing at her ear, telling her that what she had lost this time was immeasurable—impossible to have, or try to protect, ever again.

As she dragged herself into the kitchen, her cell phone sounded on the counter. It could be Cole with some news about their father's ongoing stalker situation, she thought. But, checking the ID, tears sprang to her eyes. Her finger itched to swipe the screen, accept the call. But what if she lost it and broke down?

Finally, she pushed the phone aside and crossed to the pantry. She forced down a protein shake—vanilla with blueberries, usually her favorite, although this morning it went down like gobs of tasteless sludge. After tying her shoes, she stretched her calves while trying to project positive thoughts for the coming day. Thought dictated behavior, which in turn determined mood. Picking yourself up and moving forward was without question the best way.

And yet this minute she only wanted to curl up and cry.

When her phone sounded again, Teagan set her hands over her ears and headed for her rowing machine. She didn't have any answers for Damon. He would simply have to accept it. She didn't want to—couldn't bear to—see him ever again.

Three days ago, she'd sat behind her desk and had calmly passed on her decision. His eyes had gone wide. Then an amused smile had flickered at one side of the mouth she had come to adore. But when she'd stood her ground—had asked him to leave—his jaw had tensed and his brows had drawn together.

"Tell me what's going on, Tea," he'd said. "I won't leave until you do."

Now, as she positioned herself on the machine, strapped in her feet, grabbed the ropes and eased into the flow— sliding forward, easing back, pushing with her legs, holding in her belly…already firm and flat and *empty*—

She dropped the handles. The ropes flew back and, shaking, she covered her face. She'd already cried so much, surely she was done, and yet the salty streams coursing down her cheeks wouldn't stop.

It must pass *sometime*—the constant praying and begging that she could have that chance again. Because she didn't know how much longer she could bear it...the images from that night when her greatest dream came true had turned into a nightmare. It all seemed so pointless, so gut-wrenchingly cruel. She'd been told she would never conceive. She'd learned to live with that fact. She'd pushed on and had come to accept it.

But how could she ever accept that she'd miscarried a child—Damon's baby—because now...

Nothing in the world seemed to matter.

* * * * *

If you liked Wynn's story, don't miss a single novel
in THE HUNTER PACT *series from*
Robyn Grady:
LOSING CONTROL
TEMPTATION ON HIS TERMS
All available now, from Harlequin Desire!

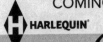
#2293 ONE GOOD COWBOY
Diamonds in the Rough • by Catherine Mann
To inherit the family business, CEO Stone McNair must prove he isn't
heartless underneath his ruthlessly suave exterior. His trial? Finding homes
for rescue dogs. His judge? The ex-fiancée who's heart he broke.

#2294 THE BLACK SHEEP'S INHERITANCE
Dynasties: The Lassiters • by Maureen Child
Suspicious of his late father's nurse when she inherits millions in his
father's will, Sage Lassiter is determined to get the truth. Even if he has
to seduce it out of her.

#2295 HIS LOVER'S LITTLE SECRET
Billionaires and Babies • by Andrea Laurence
Artist Sabine Hayes fell hard for shipping magnate Gavin Brooks, and
when it was over, she found herself pregnant. Now he's come to demand
his son—and the passion they've both denied.

#2296 A NOT-SO-INNOCENT SEDUCTION
The Kavanaghs of Silver Glen • by Janice Maynard
The sexy but stoic Liam has headed the Kavanagh family since his reckless
father's disappearance two decades ago. But meeting the innocent,
carefree Zoe awakens his passions, derailing his sense of duty.

#2297 WANTING WHAT SHE CAN'T HAVE
The Master Vintners • by Yvonne Lindsay
Her best friend's last wish was that Alexis care for her baby—and her
husband. So Alexis becomes the nanny, determined to heal this family
without falling for the one man she can't have.

#2298 ONCE PREGNANT, TWICE SHY
by Red Garnier
Wealthy Texan Garret Gage promised to protect family friend Kate just as
fiercely as her father would have. And he'd been doing just fine, until one
night of passion changes everything.

REQUEST YOUR FREE BOOKS!
2 FREE NOVELS PLUS 2 FREE GIFTS!

HARLEQUIN®

Desire

ALWAYS POWERFUL, PASSIONATE AND PROVOCATIVE

YES! Please send me 2 FREE Harlequin Desire® novels and my 2 FREE gifts (gifts are worth about $10). After receiving them, if I don't wish to receive any more books, I can return the shipping statement marked "cancel." If I don't cancel, I will receive 6 brand-new novels every month and be billed just $4.55 per book in the U.S. or $4.99 per book in Canada. That's a savings of at least 13% off the cover price! It's quite a bargain! Shipping and handling is just 50¢ per book in the U.S. and 75¢ per book in Canada.* I understand that accepting the 2 free books and gifts places me under no obligation to buy anything. I can always return a shipment and cancel at any time. Even if I never buy another book, the two free books and gifts are mine to keep forever.

225/326 HDN F4ZC

Name _____ (PLEASE PRINT) _____

Address _____ Apt. # _____

City _____ State/Prov. _____ Zip/Postal Code _____

Signature (if under 18, a parent or guardian must sign)

Mail to the **Harlequin® Reader Service:**
IN U.S.A.: P.O. Box 1867, Buffalo, NY 14240-1867
IN CANADA: P.O. Box 609, Fort Erie, Ontario L2A 5X3

Want to try two free books from another line?
Call 1-800-873-8635 or visit www.ReaderService.com.

* Terms and prices subject to change without notice. Prices do not include applicable taxes. Sales tax applicable in N.Y. Canadian residents will be charged applicable taxes. Offer not valid in Quebec. This offer is limited to one order per household. Not valid for current subscribers to Harlequin Desire books. All orders subject to credit approval. Credit or debit balances in a customer's account(s) may be offset by any other outstanding balance owed by or to the customer. Please allow 4 to 6 weeks for delivery. Offer available while quantities last.

Your Privacy—The Harlequin® Reader Service is committed to protecting your privacy. Our Privacy Policy is available online at www.ReaderService.com or upon request from the Harlequin Reader Service.

We make a portion of our mailing list available to reputable third parties that offer products we believe may interest you. If you prefer that we not exchange your name with third parties, or if you wish to clarify or modify your communication preferences, please visit us at www.ReaderService.com/consumerschoice or write to us at Harlequin Reader Service Preference Service, P.O. Box 9062, Buffalo, NY 14269. Include your complete name and address.